HER AUGUST RUSH

Bernadette Williams

Taylour Mayde Publishing

ISBN: 978-1-64136-816-2

Cover Design by Bernadette Williams and Trevis Williams
Author Photo by Victouria Williams
Editor: René Grant

ACKNOWLEDGMENTS

There comes a point in a person's life where we have to make a choice to either give up or stand and fight for what you want. I thank God that he made me to fight. The course to the finish line has been long and filled with "life". But here is proof that as long as you don't stop moving your feet, you will continue to move forward. Never give up on your dreams!

I'm grateful for my family: Trevis, Taylour, Sophia, Brent, Victouria, and my grands, April and Andrew, and for God allowing me to be a wife, mother and grandmother to them.

To my husband, Trevis, thank you for your love, support, creative help, and for the space to create. It means the world to me. I got you, wit my ....!

Victouria, thanks for the creative pointers. Although I wanted you to do more with your tremendous talent for me. Renè, thanks for your help, encouragement and work on this project. Thanks Kennetta for just being you. Turn the pages, you'll understand what I mean.

To my Dad, Clarence Grant, my Poppy, no matter the issue or my life's season, there are two things I am sure of. One, you'll love me no matter what and I'll always be your Sugar. And two, I can count on the knowledge that you have and will always expect more of me than what I consider my best. Because to you, that is just simply my norm. I love you for that.

To my spiritual parents, Pastor Karol and 1st Lady Michelle Warren, thank you for your mentorship, guidance, words of wisdom, example and love. I thank God for placing me in your spirits. You are a treasure to me.

There are so many others who have been a source of encouragement and support. I say thank you to each of you. To everyone that supports this project, thank you from the bottom of my heart and God bless you.

And finally, to my Mother, my Mommy, my friend, voice of wisdom, reason and unconditional love, Gloria Jean Brown, thank you for showing what truly loving and trusting God looks like, how loving and lifting up others works, and how powerful, empowering and peaceful quiet strength really is. I miss you and honor you with the very last period of this project.

Bernadette Williams

TABLE OF CONTENTS

Chapter One - Monday	9
Chapter Two - Friday	19
Chapter Three - Saturday	27
Chapter Four - Sunday	39
Chapter Five	41
Chapter Six	46
Chapter Seven - Monday	48
Chapter Eight - Flashback - Five Years Ago	55
Chapter Nine - Monday	65
Chapter Ten - Anthony	74
Chapter Eleven	79
Chapter Twelve - Monday - Back To The Present	83
Chapter Thirteen - Tuesday	87
Chapter Fourteen	106
Chapter Fifteen	120
Chapter Sixteen - Wednesday	128
Chapter Seventeen	135
Chapter Eighteen	144
Chapter Nineteen	154
Chapter Twenty	164
Chapter Twenty-One	170
Chapter Twenty-Two	183
Chapter Twenty-Three - Next Thursday	191
Chapter Twenty-Four	198
Chapter Twenty-Five	207
Chapter Twenty-Six	211
Chapter Twenty-Seven	218
Chapter Twenty-Eight	223
Chapter Twenty-Nine	226
Discussion Question	230

CHAPTER ONE
THURSDAY

Terry didn't sleep well last night. She never does the night before a dental appointment. She has hated the dentist since she was eight years old with her first cavity.

A most savvy entrepreneur for her age, Terry Ellis sold everything from freeze cups during the hot summers, to Jolly Ranchers and Blow Pops, to emergency school supplies to her classmates in elementary and middle school. Unfortunately, she became a victim of her success. She was sometimes her own best candy customer and ended up in the dentist chair way before time one year with a horrendous toothache. The memory of that time refreshes itself at the very sight of a dental advertisement.

Terry usually took a half day from work since she normally sweats through her blouse. All she wanted to do was curl up on her couch, grab her favorite blanket and watch a couple of shows saved on her DVR until her appetite returned and she felt like herself again.

It was a nice day in Atlanta. It rained the night before and the August heat had yet to settle back in. She rode with her windows down, enjoying the sounds of the city and the breeze blowing across her face. She was still feeling a little flushed and the cool air felt wonderful. "Thank you Lord for getting me through another dental visit."

She pulled her Mercedes into her gated community on Piedmont Road and headed down the lane toward her three level townhouse. She loved living in the end unit and having only one neighbor.

But when she got close to her destination, the sound of loud music caught her attention. That was very unusual for the middle of the day. And it became louder the closer she got to her home. This really annoyed her because she just wanted some quiet time to finish winding down.

"Who is playing their music that loud?" she wondered out loud. She thought her neighbor Eric was out of town. But he must have returned early. "He's just gonna have to turn that down so I can catch my nap."

When Terry pulled into the garage beneath her townhouse and stepped out of her car she stopped cold. "What the..?" The music was coming from upstairs. From her house.

She slipped off her shoes, unlocked the door leading from the garage and slowly walked up the stairs with her taser in one hand and pepper spray in the other. A real criminal wouldn't advertise his presence so she believed she'd be able to handle whatever was going on. Her heart was already pounding but she was confident in her self defense training. Being a woman in the Atlanta single scene, she had to be ready to drop a fool if she had to. But what she saw when she stepped out of the kitchen into the dining room made her head spin.

There he was, her boyfriend, Mr. Reginald Lockwood, stock broker extraordinaire, perfectionist, critic of all he didn't create and genius in his own mind. She couldn't believe it. He was actually sitting in her house doing drugs like some undercover, high class junkie.

"Reggie!" she yelled.

His head jerked up and a look of sheer panic swept over his face. He reached for the remote and snapped the stereo off. "Fool!" Terry took one step and Reggie jumped back so quickly she would have laughed if she wasn't so angry.

"Terry, I can explain!" he pleaded with his hands raised against the threat of her drawn taser.

"What? What is there to explain? Your crazy behind is sniffing drugs up your nose in my house. And on the most precious piece of furniture that I own! That was my great grandmother's, you fool!"

"But!"

"But Nothing! You, Mr. Lockwood are done! You self righteous, egotistical, lying S.O.B!!! How could you?" She was barely containing her emotions.

"Terry. Look Honey, I..." Reggie tried to calm her down.

"Honey!? Honey implies something sweet is going on. And right now, I am pissed as all get out! Who the hell do you think you are bringing that mess up in here? Have you lost your damned mind?!"

Terry stared at the white dust on her great-grandmother's antique coffee table and felt another wave of heat rush over her. She took another step in his direction and raised her pepper spray in his direction just to prove how mad she was.

Reggie opened his mouth to speak but was cut short by Terry when another thought came to mind.

"Wait a minute. Wait a damn minute." College days, tear the paper off the walls Terry started to show through. A string of curse words lined themselves up in her mind and they were cocked and ready to fly. Suddenly she felt hot all over.

Wait! I can't. She took a deep breath. I'm gonna hold it together.

"I know, I just know you ain't been bringing that sh---, crap up in my house all this time. No. No. No! No! Hell to the naw. I just know you ain't. But just in case, I'm bout to break your ass off something I know you can't handle." She couldn't hold it any longer. She locked eyes with Reggie and made her taser crackle.

Reggie grabbed his jacket and swept everything he could off the table into it. In the time he'd known her, he'd never seen Terry in such a state. He wasn't about to hang around to see what happened next.

"I'm sorry Terry!" was all he could get out while backing towards the front door.

"I don't want to hear another damn word out of your mouth! Just get the hell out! Now!" Terry yelled and kicked her foot in his direction, hoping to make contact. That wouldn't have been so threatening except for the fact that he knew she was working on her blue belt in karate.

Reggie's eyes widened. After Terry got saved, she worked very hard to never use any kind of profanity, let alone threaten anyone with physical harm. That was confirmation that the situation was much worse than he thought just moments before. He ripped the door open and ran down the stairs to his car parked around the corner. Terry watched him peel out of the parking lot, her heart beating a mile a minute.

After she closed her front door, Terry just stood there staring at her living room replaying what just went down. If it had not happened in front of her, she would never have believed Reggie was into drugs of any kind. Straight laced and safe is all she knew of him. He was totally not what she envisioned she'd end up with in college, but he fit into the corporate mold she had created and was starting to fill.

How could he do this? What was he thinking? She got angry all over again. "What the f....? Woo Lord!" She braced herself on the table near the door. "You gone have to help me right now. And I do mean Right NOW! Ooo, What was I thinking?"

She stood for minute in silence, breathing slowly to calm herself again before she went to the kitchen to get cleanser and paper towels to remove any traces of Reggie's transgression. She paused in the middle of scrubbing to steady her nerves and thank God for keeping her far enough away from Reggie that she couldn't actually hurt him. That would have only made matters worse.

She had just finished scrubbing the table and was setting up the vacuum to make sure there was nothing left in the carpet when the phone rang. She didn't want to answer any questions right now. But if it was her best friend Leighann, she knew she would have to. Leighann always seemed to know just when something wasn't quite right with her. She decided to answer just in case it was her. She'd just call again until she did. And Terry suddenly wanted to tell it all.

"Hello."

"Terry, you were supposed to call me as soon as you got home. You know the routine." Leighann immediately laid into her. "How long have you been home?"

"About 30 minutes. Maybe a little longer," Terry answered as she flopped down on the sofa.

Leighann didn't like the sound of her voice. "What's wrong?" When terry didn't answer right away she took a deep breath and asked again, more forcefully. "Terry, what is wrong and do I need to be there now?"

"Yes. But don't run any lights. I'll tell you all about it when you get here." Terry didn't want to cry and she knew she would if she started talking right now. Leighann did not need another reason to speed with two tickets just last month.

"Give me fifteen minutes," and the phone went silent.

Terry grabbed the vacuum and finished cleaning up. True to her word, Leighann knocked, unlocked and entered through the front door just short of her promised time. "Terry, where are you?"

"I'm in here," Terry called from the couch. Leighann took a seat next to her and took her hand.

"So, tell me what's going on. Did your appointment go bad?" Terry took a deep breath and told Leighann what happened. Leighann's eyes grew bigger the more she talked, and Terry got angry all over again. She was pacing the floor by the time she finished.

"And now I have to trash a two hundred dollar vacuum cleaner because I don't want to take the chance of spreading anything he may have spilled all over the rest of my house. And God forbid anything happens that would cause my house to be searched and traces of drugs are found here. I know, I know. I'm reaching here. But there have been people who have been taken down with less." Terry took another deep breath and sat down again next to Leighann.

Leighann sat there in silence. There was only once in all the time Terry had known her that Leighann had no words. And that was the day her mother passed away. For two days she walked around in silence and Terry shadowed her fearing she was having a breakdown.

After a few moments of silence, Leighann cleared her throat. "I'm sitting here trying to figure out how you did it."

Terry turned to her puzzled. "How did I do what?"

Leighann stood and spun around with her hands on her hips. "How the hell did you keep from shooting that bum?!"

Terry opened her mouth but didn't get a word out before Leighann paced past her and continued her tirade.

"I knew it. And I told you so. This man found every excuse in the book to cancel every time we were supposed to meet him. And you know why? Do you wanna know why? Cause he's shifty and he's sneaky. I always wondered about him anyway!"

She stopped pacing and looked Terry in the eye before she went on. "I told you something was wrong. He's just busy you said. He already had plans. Always something! I bet your behind will listen to me the next time I tell you I smell a rat!" Leighann took her seat again holding her head high with "I Told You So" written all over her face.

Terry got up from the couch ready to defend herself from yet another lecture from her best friend. She loved her but hated when she became Mother Leigh.

"Look, I need your support not your criticism. And don't you dare sit there all superior because I remember all too well Jason Maxwell, artist extraordinaire, bum magnificent!"

She knew how to stop Leighann. She hated this skeleton that turned her life upside down.

"You did not have to go there," Leighann said quietly.

Terry pushed on. "Like I said, I need your support. And you, of all people, should understand what it is like to deal with being betrayed by someone you put your trust in. So, sorry I hurt your feelings, but I am not going to be beat up on right now. I haven't even had the chance to come down from that damned appointment and I have to deal with this Reggie crap. I can not take any more drama right this minute." By now, Terry was practically yelling.

"Terry, I'm sorry but you know how I get when some joker thinks he can just do what he wants to one of my friends." Leighann defended her behavior.

Just then, the doorbell rang. Terry opened the door to find Angela standing poised to ring again.

"Oh, baby girl are you alright?" Angela wrapped her in her arms. "Leighann called me on her way over to let me know something else had gone down. I don't know what happened but I'm here now. Where is Leigh?"

"In here."

Angela went to the living room and took a seat between Terry and Leighann. "Now, tell me what happened."

"A snake in the grass sniffin' dirt, that's what!" Leighann chimed in.

Terry rolled her eyes, then took a deep breath and started from the top. She watched Angela's eyes widen, while her mouth opened and closed in disbelief. Her head spun from face to face looking for one of them to say "gotcha" or something.

"I cannot believe it," Angela said shaking her head.

"Girl, If I had not walked in on him, I wouldn't believe it either. And, I know Leigh, if I had listened to you when you expressed concerns, maybe I wouldn't be in this situation."

"That's right, I told you so." Leighann had to get one more in.

Terry and Angela both rolled their eyes at Leighann.

"I'm hungry. Anyone for snapper?" Terry rose from her seat and headed towards the kitchen.

"Why are you changing subject?" Leighann antagonized.

"I said, I'm hungry. And I don't want to talk about it anymore. Now, do you want snapper or are you eating at your house?"

Angela knew that, although she loved Terry dearly, Leighann would take this as a challenge and strike back. She couldn't let that happen after all that already went on today.

"Look! Leighann don't get nasty. And Terry, cool it!"

"What?!" Terry looked at Angela angrily. "I have just had the day from hell and she is supposed to be here in support of me, not tearing me down and taking shots. And if I wasn't saved, I'd have a lot more interesting things to say about all of this and her attitude." Terry turned questioning eyes to Leighann. "I thought we came to an understanding just a little while ago."

"Look, whatever. I did what I came to do. Bet your butt will listen to me next time." Leighann stood, grabbed her purse and headed towards the door.

"Leighann. Leigh!" Angela called after her.

Terry stood in the middle of the floor with her arms folded across her chest.

"Leighann Marie Collins!" Leighann hated when Terry used her whole name. She stopped cold with her hand on the doorknob ready to make a quick exit. She turned back to give Terry a piece of her mind and burst out in laughter at the look on Terry's face.

Terry and Angela tried to keep their composure but couldn't hold in their laughter. The three of them laughed until their stomachs hurt and they were out of breath.

"You know I hate when you do that." Leighann eyed Terry trying to make a stern face through her laughter.

"I know. Why do you think I did it?" Terry replied with a satisfied look on her face.

"Cause you are evil. Come here." The ladies embraced, making up like they always have since their days in college.

They moved into the kitchen and carried on with preparing an early supper while carefully keeping the conversation Reggie free.

They emptied a bottle of chardonnay that magically appeared after one of Leighann's famous "I'll be right back" moments. That always meant something interesting was about to happen. The atmosphere was just right for Terry to relax and make it through the rest of her night. She only ate about half of her dinner. And not much for drinking anymore, Terry only consumed about half her glass, as did Angela. But Leighann made sure the bottle didn't go to waist.

"Y'all don't waste my wine. This is one of my good bottles," Leighann ordered. "I know ya'll loving Jesus and all but even he turned water into wine."

"Alright Leigh, that's enough," Angela spoke up. "Don't mess with my Lord."

"I keep telling her not to play with Him. One day she's going to call on Him and He's going to say, Louise who." Terry chimed in through her laughter.

"Ha Ha. Not funny T. I know God. We have a very special relationship. You just wouldn't understand. I'm a work in progress. Don't judge me." Terry and Angela looked at each other and burst out into laughter.

They reminisced and joked each other until Angela felt she was ok to drive home. She was a true lightweight. The only thing missing from the impromptu party was their fourth wheel Kristine. Around 8:30, Angela and Leighann said their goodbyes and left Terry with wishes for pleasant dreams and a restful night.

"Now, if you need backup tonight, you call me. You know I'm always packing," Leighann offered.

Terry looked at Leighann and shook her head. "What did Uncle Sam do to my sweet friend? I'm going to start calling you Leigh Annie Oakley."

"Whatever chick. I simply found something I enjoy. A lot! I aim straight and never miss. On that you can count." Leighann struck a Charlie's Angels pose, causing another round of laughter to fill the room. That girl could work her last nerve, but Terry couldn't imagine not having her as a part of her life.

Terry closed the door quietly behind them and turned to look at her empty living room. It once again seemed peaceful. Her extended family, her girls, saved the day. God knew who to put in her life. No matter what has come her way, her girls have always been able to get her through the madness.

CHAPTER TWO
FRIDAY

It's Friday morning and today is the day to close the Tadashi deal. Terry was up early and ready for war, if need be.

She and her partner Anthony Broder have been working on this contract for six months and it was finally ready to be signed. They were going to take over all aspects of advertising for one of the largest electronics manufacturing distributors this side of the Atlantic. This deal meant television, radio and print both here and abroad, in twenty languages. And that was only the first stage. After the first wave of the campaign was successful, the contract contained a provision to expand to a second branch of the parent conglomerate. The work on the second branch alone had the potential to triple her income. She had to be sure that she was on point today.

Terry spent an hour in prayer and meditation last night which soothed her spirit and cleared her mind. She didn't plan on being up so late, but it was easy to lose track of time when she found her peaceful place in God. Thoughts of Reggie were pushed far away for another day and now she was able to refocus her energy on the task at hand.

Most people considered wearing a blue or black power suit for heavy negotiations, but Terry wasn't average and refused to dress that way. Public relations was her business so she made a point to always stand out. She dressed in her white tailored Carlos Meile dress over a high collared Alfa tailored shirt with oversized cuffs and her platinum cufflinks. She slipped her feet into her Tracy Reese Levi sandals and stood to admire God's perfection. "I know you are not a respecter of persons, but Father God, as I look upon your creation this morning, I do believe I have to be one of your favorites." It's amazing how prayer, a good night's sleep and the feel of quality against your skin made your morning just feel brighter. "Father, I will earnestly endeavor to remain humble today," she proclaimed. Smiling at the confidence she saw on her face, she prayed seriously, "God, thank you for getting me through this week. You are my joy and my strength and I look to see your glory today. I know you've equipped me to deal with whatever comes my way today. And I will walk in victory. I love you. Amen."

Terry took one last inventory of her briefcase and contract package. She was not going to take a chance of leaving anything behind. Closing this deal should only take about an hour if it that long. And she was ready to move through the process quickly and orderly.

She slid into the front seat of her Mercedes and began the journey to solidify the biggest deal of her career. She was 15 minutes into her drive and on the phone with Anthony when she heard a rumble and her car started to shake a bit. "Hold on Anthony," she stopped talking to listen.

"Okay." He waited silently, unaware a situation was brewing.

"Aw man. Anthony, I think I caught a flat. I may have to call you back." She was going to push to her stop two exits away but the rumble was getting louder so she pulled off on the first exit she reached. She didn't even make it to the light at the top of the ramp. As soon as she slowed down, the car pulled treacherously to the right. She carefully pulled as far off the road as she could without tilting the car towards the down side of the ramp.

"Dang it Anthony. I do not need this today." She told him where she was and to call the nearest courier service. She'd leave the car and ride with them if she had to and the tow truck would have to wait if it didn't reach her first. Terry grabbed her car's documents and stepped out of her car. Clutching her briefcase and phone, she was preparing to walk the rest of the way up the hill. She walked around the front of the car to take a look at the damaged wheel and was surprised at how bad it was.

But it was nothing compared to the chill of fear that ran through her when she looked past her car to see another vehicle flying up the ramp with the driver bent towards the passenger's seat. This car wasn't slowing down. Terry let out a terrifying scream. She called out the only thing that came to mind. "JESUS!" Just then the other driver looked up and Terry saw the panic in his eyes. She took only a few steps backwards before she tripped and he jerked his steering wheel. But it wasn't in time to miss the impact with her car. It sent her Mercedes sliding down the embankment and his Acura into a spin across the exit into the guardrail.

Terry was sitting in a trembling ball when the lady from the Nissan behind the Acura ran to her side. "It's alright. The car missed you." Terry lifted her head and peeled her eyes open. Her eyes fell to the marks on the gravel and in the grass in front of her. Yes, her car missed her, but it was pushed pretty close to her before it slid down the hill.

"Can you stand?" the lady asked.

"I don't know." She felt stuck in this ball with her bag pinned to her chest as if she expected it to shield her from being hurt.

Terry noticed then the commotion to her left. The driver of the Acura had made it out of the rear passenger side window of his car with the help of people from the traffic blocked by the accident. He was also visibly shaken. But that only irritated her. He should be shook up. She slowly stood up from the ground still trembling. But didn't hesitate to thank God for keeping her safe.

"I'm so sorry. Oh God, I am so sorry. Are you alright?" The guilty man approached Terry. When she didn't respond right away, he turned to the lady that helped her up. "Is she ok? I saw her on the ground. Please tell me she's ok!"

"I'm not a doctor. You'll have to ask whoever comes to help you. There's a fire station close by so they should be here really soon," the lady responded.

Terry spoke up. "What were you thinking? You could've killed me!" The reality of what she just said hit her and she started shaking again.

They could hear the sirens approaching.

"I am so sorry," the man said softly with tears welling up in his eyes. "I was just trying to surprise my wife with flowers this morning and they, they tipped over. I only looked down for a second." He paused, and starting shaking his head, staring down at the ground. He looked up into Terry's eyes and said softly, "It was only a moment." Then he sunk to the ground with tears streaming down his face. As upset as Terry was, she was even more perplexed.

"Is that how easy, how quickly it happened?" he whispered. Then he dropped his head into his hands and let his tears flow freely.

Now, Terry was really confused. "What the heck?" Wasn't she the one who almost lost her life.

The emergency vehicles arrived quickly. Someone led a paramedic over to Terry and they took her over to one of the trucks to take her vitals and assess her physical status. Terry looked over to where the man who could have taken everything from her was talking to the EMT and suddenly she knew who this man was. Lewis. Jason. No, Jarod Lewis. Seven months ago his daughter was killed in a car accident and he went on a campaign of no mercy for the driver of the vehicle. Wendy Lewis was his daughter's name. She was twenty-three and headed back to law school after a visit home. Now she understood. She was still angry, but at least she felt for certain that this person was genuine in his remorse. And he could definitely understand the impact on another person's life his actions could have had. Forgiveness was already finding its way out of her heart.

"Excuse me, are either of you Terry Ellis?" A policeman escorting a man with a metal case approached her.

"I am," Terry answered and immediately her heart began to race. She didn't remember when she put down her briefcase and phone and this had to be the courier.

"This guy is from a courier service sent to meet you." The Police officer left the courier with her and went back to finish his work.

"Hi. I was sent by Anthony Broder." He read from his notes.

"Yes, um, hold on. At the moment, I don't know where I put my briefcase," you could hear the stress in her voice.

The paramedic reached into the truck and produced her case. "Is this what you are looking for?"

"Oh, thank God. Thank you so much." She opened her case and pulled out the envelope with the contract in it and handed it to the courier. She double checked the details of the delivery and made sure that the instructions to confirm delivery were firmly in place.

Just as the courier left, another police officer approached her to complete his interview.

When he was done, Terry picked up her phone and called Anthony. She filled him in on the details of the last forty minutes. She let him know that the contract was picked up but he already knew. The service was instructed to notify him of both the pickup and delivery. He was also watching the news and had seen the accident on TV. She had 21 missed calls from him.

Anthony asked if she wanted him to call the girls and she quickly told him no. "No! I don't want anyone panicking. You know how Angela is." She would be fine and would call them when she was on her way from the hospital back to the city.

Terry provided all the information that she needed to for the wrecker to take her car before she let the EMT's know she was ready to head for the hospital. But before they were able to leave, Jarod made his way over to her again. "Ma'am, I am so sorry. You have no idea how sorry I am and how thankful I am that you are alright." He handed her his card and told her, "If you ever need anything, and I mean anything, please call me. Here is all the information you need to have your car taken care of. Call me if you have any problems at all." Terry told him she would and then left. Calling his insurance company was going to be first on her list after she called Tadashi's office to make sure her package was delivered.

At the hospital Jarod's wife, Patrice, found her. And, to Terry's surprise, embraced her. She spent a few minutes talking with her and telling her how sad it was that this happened but how grateful she was that Terry is okay. And she also shared that her husband's heart had been healed from his deeply rooted anger. "He can now see for himself how one small thing can change someone's entire world. The void left by our daughter's death will never be filled. But at least now, he can let go of his resentment against the young lady responsible for her death. There is nothing quite like a personal confrontation with responsibility. I've been praying for him to move on and now he can. He's already made a call to accept her apology." Patrice took Terry's hands in hers. "I hope that you can truly accept Jarod's."

Patrice also handed her a business card and on the back she had written her personal number with the same instruction that if she ever needed anything, to call on them. Before she left, she assured Terry that everything with her car would be taken care of quickly.

Anthony sent a car to pick Terry up from the hospital and take her home. She wanted to go to the office but the driver was told to take her straight home and not to divert. And to make sure Terry couldn't change destinations in route, Anthony threatened to remove the car service from the company's endorsed roster if he did.

Needless to say, she gave Anthony an ear full when she called him from home to confirm delivery of the contract to Tadashi. Although she made her feelings well known, after the stress of the last forty-eight hours, she could use an afternoon of quiet. So she surrendered, "Alright. Call me if you need me."

"Will do. Get some rest." Anthony hung up.

Terry slipped off her shoes and dialed Angela's office. It took her fifteen minutes to convince Angela that she was ok and there was no need for her to drop what she was doing.

"Angela, I said I am fine. My release papers say no medication needed and I could return to normal activities without restriction. Alright!"

"You don't have to yell Ma'am. I'm just trying to look out for you."

"I know. I'm just going to make something to eat, spend a little time on my laptop, get a couple of things done around here and make it an early night. Is that alright with you Mother?"

"Don't be such a smart mouth. I'm going to let that slide because of the stress you've had to deal with this week. But make no mistake, next week your behind is mine if you get outta line," Angela quipped.

After a moment of silence, they both burst into laughter. Angela's straight laced personality and hood did not mix.

"Girl bye. Just let the girls know I am ok and update them on everything for me please."

"Yes ma'am."

"I can't take Leighann right now. I'm going to take a little quiet time and catch a nap. Suddenly I just want to lie down."

"Alright sweetheart. Call me if you need anything."

"I will."

Terry did just what she said. Other than the call to the insurance company, she spoke once with Anthony and then Kayla that afternoon. She knew she could count on them to handle everything at the office. But around three, her mind slipped into thoughts of the day before. She felt this heaviness begin to overcome her. It was odd because it felt more like disappointment than loss of someone you were in a relationship with. But then again, was she really disappointed? At that moment, she couldn't put a definite title on how she felt.

 "Best to shake it off," she told herself. She jumped up, changed and took her laptop to her treadmill and work and walked until she was tired.

The rest of her evening passed quietly. Angela called to check on her before turning in for the night.

"Hey. Do you need anything?" Angela asked through a yawn.

"No. I'm fine. The quiet time was good. I got a lot done." Terry reported. "I think I'm just going to watch a movie and then go to sleep."

"Alright. Have a good night. Sleep well."

"Good night Angela."

By the time the movie was over, the TV was watching her.

CHAPTER THREE
SATURDAY

Terry opened her eyes to the beam of light shining past the edge of the blinds.

"Uuumm." Terry loved Saturday mornings. Saturday was usually the only day she made sure there was absolutely nothing scheduled before ten thirty a.m. just so she could wake up like this. When she got good and ready. She stretched, yawned, then turned over and snuggled her face into her soft pillow. She took a deep breath and felt that wonderful melting sensation flow through her body.

She started to drift off again into quiet nothingness, wrapped in the fragrant warmth of her plush down comforter. But just before everything faded, Reggie's face popped into her head and her eyes flew open. She shut them tight again, took another deep breath and tried hard to relax and change her thoughts back to the dream she was having, her favorite song, a story, shopping, shoes, and then her neighbor's new baby. But nothing worked. She felt her heartbeat speed up and her body tense. "Damn!" She threw the covers back and stomped to the bathroom.

Terry washed her hands and splashed water on her face. She looked in the mirror and whispered to herself, "It's going to be just fine. You've got it together. You've got your friends, family and your work. And nothing has happened that you can't recover from." Then she whispered a prayer. "God, help me get through this day so I can make it to church service tomorrow. I need a Word and refreshing from you. Damn is a small curse, but it came out way too easy. And we both know, I do not need to start that habit again."

Somewhat soothed, she patted her face dry as she went to answer the phone by the bed. Dropping onto her plush comforter, she hit the talk button.

"Hello?"

"I want you dressed and ready to accompany me to this wedding by

11:30am. It's an hour drive and I want to get a good seat," ordered her friend Krystine. Terry blinked hard and took the phone from her ear and wished the woman at the other end of the line could see the stare she was giving her. The youngest of her four-woman crew, Krystine Owens was bossy, blunt, demanding and a ham like you wouldn't believe. Terry fully intended to tell her no way but she didn't have a chance since Krystine was still barking out orders. "The wedding does not begin until 2:30pm but we need to get the best seats for the best photo opportunities. You know the drill."

Terry closed her eyes and took a deep breath. "I am not in the mood to put on a show today Krys. After the week I've had I…"

Krystine, quickly cutting her off, simply said, "11:30 I will be at your front door. Be dressed in something cute but sexy, preferably a neutral color and maybe a strappy sandal. Bummer on the week, but you cannot stay shut in." Krystine paused just long enough for Terry to open her mouth to speak, but of course she wouldn't let her utter a single word. "You know I get what I want!" Krystine declared.

"Damn" for the second time that morning Terry swore and hung up the phone since she knew Krystine was already gone. "May as well," she said heading to the shower. But if she had to go, she was going all out. This was a celebrity wedding Krystyne had been advertising to her friends for the last three weeks. And she was not about to be the "who?" girl of the group. It was only 9:23 and she could make miracles happen in two hours.

Shortly before her deadline, Terry stood before her full-length mirror admiring her work. She chose the perfect champagne colored knee length dress that hugged her waist but draped seductively in soft folds around her hips. Turning slightly to check the low cut scooped back, she took in how that drew just a little extra attention to her backside. She liked it. She chose her gold slingbacks with the soft shimmer and jeweled ankle strap. She felt beautiful. A little extra beautiful. And after all the drama this week, she needed that. "Krys had better watch herself today", she smiled seductively at her reflection.

She checked her watch and at 11:30 am on the dot Terry walked to her door and swung it open just before Krystine's finger could touch the doorbell. She struck a pose with a raised brow and sexy pouted lips. Krystine gave her the once over and blurted out, "that don't look

Christian to me!", then turned and descended the stairs, strutting back to her Mercedes where Angela and Leighann were waiting. She hated it when anyone looked as good as she did.

Terry turned to lock her door with a satisfied smile. If Krystine had a problem with her outfit, she knew she was on point. Terry slid into the back seat with a "Hello ladies". She smiled at her friends. "Lovely day isn't it?" She declared when she caught Krystine's eye in the rearview mirror.

"Are you looking for another man already?" Leighann quizzed sarcastically.

Terry's smile froze in place and she turned to Leighann sitting beside her. "No. But every man, and a few jealous women, will have their attention on me. Thank you. And do not start." Effectively shutting down Leighann, she turned her focus to Angela and Krystine. "So Krys, who's the lucky bride you're trying to outshine this week?"

Angela jumped in proclaiming, "You know it doesn't even matter who it is, because she will swear she's a dog next to Krys". This sparked the first of several topics of discussion that made the drive time pass quickly.

Before they knew it, Krystine's Mercedes was pulling into the church parking lot which was already half full. Krystine took the very first spot she saw, took a quick look at her face and told her passengers, "Let's go girls. We've already missed the money shot seats, so stay close. We have to move quickly. My face needs to be in at least one of Donna Craven's wedding photos."

"Yes sergeant," they chimed in unison.

Krystine was three strides away when she stopped suddenly and turned to face her companions with the order, "And don't you dare embarrass me when we go through security,....Leighann."

"Why do you have to call my name?" Leighann questioned with mock innocence.

Krystine crossed her arms and raised a brow.

"Oh, alright!"   Leighann reached back into the car and removed something from her handbag. "Satisfied?"

Krystine said, "I guess I'll find out shortly." And with that she turned and proceeded towards the church waving the girls along. "Let's go Ladies!"

Terry was the first to catch up and match her stride. She looked too good to walk behind Krystine today. She knew she was at her best. She could tell from the look Krystine gave her when she opened her front door this morning that Krystine was truly bothered by how good she looked. Terry smiled and thought to herself, "She'll just have to deal with it. I'm not pulling any punches today."

Getting through security was uneventful. Krystine went through first and watched quietly while her friends worked their way through. Satisfied that everything was going well, Krystine, with her companions in tow, went on her mission to find the seats in the room that would catch the most flashes. Bride's side? Groom's side? It only mattered that the photographers shot her good side.

All the aisle seats were taken. "Dang-it," Krystine mumbled when she saw the seats left to choose from. "Well, the lighting is better on the left so let's go." They sat eight rows back on the left side of the church. Of course Krystine had to get as close to the aisle as possible. But Terry made sure she was right next to her.

The ladies settled in to people watch while the church filled and show time approached. Terry thought she had the perfect seat until the empty space in front of her was filled by a woman wearing a huge first lady hat in pale pink. She thought she'd be able to work around her until her twin wearing a pastel blue look alike sat next to her. "The perfect movie seat. Can't see a thing," Terry whispered.

At 2:15 the musicians began to play, setting the mood for the ceremony. Everyone settled down and listened to the musicians. And then Musiq, the star vocalist, stood to do the opening song. Terry loved Soul Child's style.

So far, the wedding coordinator impressed Terry even though she'd never met her. Half way through his rendition of "You and I", the reverend came in from the back followed by the groom and best man.

Of course, Terry barely caught the tops of their heads and a leg or two through the sea of netting and flowers. Oh well, she'd get a good look when everyone stood and shifted a bit.

The doors at the back of the church then opened to reveal the bridesmaids in luxurious silk mauve dresses in various styles. All eyes were on the twelve couples that walked the aisle. Each duo posed midway down the aisle. It was like a mini fashion show. Even the flower girls walked the runway with attitude in their sparkling white finery and glass slippers. The third flower girl wasn't even in place before the doors opened again to draw all eyes and cameras to the bride's grand entrance and everyone rose.

There were so many people there, only the ones sitting on the inner half of the pews received more than a glimpse of the bride as she glided by on the arm of the handsomest older man in the building. Leighann whispered to Terry "Dang, daddy is fine. Wonder if he has a single son?" Terry just rolled her eyes. The gown, what Terry saw of it, was stunning. Krystine had informed them on the ride in that the bride favored Pnina Tornai.

Just as Donna and her father reached the altar, the sea of hats standing in front of her parted and Terry could see the groom step towards the approaching couple. Everything but the picture before Terry faded away. She suddenly felt hot all over and there was no sound, only the silent movie playing in front of her.

Everyone stood while the reverend took a few moments to share what marriage means. Angela leaned over to Terry to comment on the bride's gown but Terry didn't even acknowledge her. Angela looked carefully at Terry and knew something wasn't right.

The reverend asked, "And who gives this woman to be wed?"

"I do," answered Mr. Craven and he went to his seat. When the reverend announced, "You may be seated", the women in front of Terry descended and she was able to see the wedding party without obstruction. It took several seconds for the crowd to settle down again and Terry took in all that was before her. Angela pulled her hand and ordered, "Terry, sit down." Terry's purse hit the floor. Drawing Leighann's attention, she quietly quizzed, "What is wrong with her?"

Angela looked up to see what had Terry's attention. "Oh no." She looked at Krystine's angry face and whispered as calmly as she could, "We have to leave. Now!"

Krystine looked at Angela like she had just lost her mind. "No! Make her sit down." Krystine pasted on a smile covered in mock politeness.

Angela looked up pointedly at the front of the church and said, "That," nodding at the altar, "is Reggie." She'd only been in his presence once, and then for only about thirty seconds before he ran away. But she remembered him vividly.

Krystine and Leighann's eyes snapped to the front of the church in stark disbelief.

By this time, the preacher had moved on and was posing the question ending with, "let him speak now or forever hold his peace?" The preacher's voice held a question at the rumble of voices that had grown very noticeable by this time.

All eyes turned to see what the commotion was. When their eyes met, Reggie's face turned a shade of red Terry had never seen before and would never forget. She felt frozen. She wanted to run, scream, and throw something between his eyes, but she just could not move.

Angela had to do something. She looked around and took her cell phone from her purse, jumped up and began waving it next to Terry and said the first reasonable thing that came to mind. "We apologize, but she just received a disturbing text about her mother and we have to leave. She, she's in a bit of shock." Angela was pushing against Leighann and pulling at Terry to move them towards the end of the pew as she talked. "Please forgive the interruption. You make a gorgeous bride Donna. God bless your union." And with that, Angela rushed down the outside aisle behind Leighann nearly dragging Terry behind her. Krystine quickly pursued, making sure she picked up Terry's purse on the way. She was not coming back to face this crowd.

At the altar, Reggie's heart was beating so fast he felt like he was about to go into cardiac arrest. He fought with everything in him to keep his composure. He turned to faced his bride-to-be again. And, with as straight of a face as he could muster, asked Donna, "Are you alright?" At the same time, he was wondering if she could hear his heart pounding. He nearly lost it when he turned around and saw Terry standing there. At his wedding of all places. He felt like he was dripping wet with sweat, but he played it cool and smiled gently in the face of his young starlet bride. He worked hard convincing her to keep their relationship private and his name out of the news until the very last minute.

"Donna?"

"I'm alright." She took a deep breath. Donna was so sweet, Reggie almost felt ashamed for his deceit.

"I'm sure she'll be okay. Now, shall we?" he asked with a slight bow.

"We shall." Donna, taking a moment to steady her nerves, replied with her glowing smile. Then she turned to her matron of honor to make sure everything was still in its proper place. Reggie turned and saw the question on Mark's face. His best man and best friend since childhood knew things about Reggie that could possibly make him a small fortune. But then, Reggie was privy to all of his secrets too and he would not dare cross that line. All Reggie could do was close his eyes and take a quick calming breath himself. When he opened them again, he knew from Mark's expression that he had some explaining to do, after the ceremony. But right now his bride and the reverend were waiting and the show must go on.

Just outside the door, Terry stopped following and pushed past Angela and ran for the restroom. She couldn't hold her stomach any longer.

Terry barely made it into the stall in time. Angela stood guard to make sure Terry didn't make a mess. Leighann and Krystine paced the room exchanging looks of amazement and disbelief. Leighann had to say something.

"What the f.."

"Hey! Hey! Hey! We are in a church!" Krystine cut her off.

Leighann really wanted to explode back into the sanctuary and set something off but she wasn't going to embarrass her best friend even more than she already was. The tension in the room was so thick you needed a chainsaw to cut through it.

Then Krystine couldn't keep it in any longer. "I don't get it. Why would ...?"

"Now is not the time." Angela interrupted her. "We've got to get Terry out of here before anyone comes nosing around. Krystine, get the car to the front door. Leigh, make sure no one comes in." Angela turned her attention back to Terry as another wave of nausea hit. Angela was a rock, rubbing Terry's back for comfort like her mother would. But Angela's sense of urgency soon kicked in again and she asked, "Terry, can you get up?" Terry nodded and rose with Angela's help and walked over to the sink to rinse her mouth. Leighann cracked open the door to make sure the hallway was clear. She gave Angela a nod and after a final check, Angela led Terry out of the ladies room on a bee line to the front exit.

Krystine was just pulling up to the door when they walked out. They deposited Terry in her seat and sped out of the parking lot before the usher that was headed their way could reach the door.

The ladies rode for about five minutes before anyone would break the silence. "Is everyone alright?" Angela knew they were all shaken but she couldn't help herself.

Krystine and Leighann spoke at the same time. "What do you think?" "Are you kidding me?"

Angela, further frustrated, simply sat back in her seat and put her hand over her eyes, "I am getting a headache." Silence again took over for several minutes.

"Pull over." All eyes turned to Terry.

"Are you alright? Are you feeling sick again?" Angela asked Terry.

"Please, do not get sick in my car!" Krystine ordered.

"Girl, get over your car. Terry needs you to pull over." Leighann had to put Krystine in her place. "Just do what she asked you to. Bump this Mercedes."

Krystine was not going to be outdone in her own car. "I know you are not telling me to get over anything as bad as you are stuck on yourself. Furthermore…"

Krystine didn't get to finish her sentence. Angela had to stop this madness.

"Ladies, quiet! Right now is not about either of you. We have to get our sister home. Now cut it out or I promise I will not be responsible for what goes down next!" Angela's outburst only flamed the fire that had sparked between Krystine and Leighann. The argument continued and got louder and louder until Terry couldn't take anymore.

"PULL OVER!!!" Terry screamed at the top of her lungs. In the confined space, her voice startled her arguing friends. Krystine immediately found a spot to pull over. Terry swung the door open before the car came to a complete stop. She jumped out of the car and headed into a restaurant three doors down from where they stopped.

The three of them sat in silence for a moment before Leighann got out to follow her, "I'll bring her back."

By the time Leighann walked through the door, Terry was lifting a shot glass to her lips. Leighann was amazed at how fast Terry was moving. Terry threw back the shot and bit the lemon she was holding. Leighann's heart skipped a beat when she heard Terry order, "Another double please."

Leighann approached the bar wondering what she should say. The last time she saw Terry take shots was not a good day, for either of them.

"Terry? Terry, what are you doing?" Terry looked Leighann in the eye, licked the salt from her hand, tossed back her second tequila and turned away to gauge how much pain she still felt. It had been several years since she tasted anything more than half a glass of wine on any one occasion, so she expected the alcohol to make quick work on her system.

Leighann touched her arm but she pulled away. She didn't want to hear anything sensible right now. She just wanted to be numb. The tequila was quickly taking effect but it wasn't enough. Terry looked into the mirror over the back of the bar and wondered, "God why did Reggie lie to me like this? How could I not know?" She knew she was beautiful but not just because of her looks. She was a good person with a kind heart. She had the drive to succeed and pushed others do the same. "I don't deserve this," she whispered to her reflection. "Why?" A tear rolled down her cheek.

Leighann moved to put her arm around her shoulders but Terry shifted away. "No. Your pity is not what I need right now." Terry, holding up two fingers, nodded at the bartender, who placed two shot glasses of tequila in front of her.

"Terry you don't have to do this. We're here for you and we'll help you get through this." While Leighann talked, Terry saw Angela in the mirror coming through the door and she knew that Angela would take her away before the alcohol had completed its task. So, she made haste and swallowed her third and fourth shot of tequila, before Angela reached her side.

"Leighann! I thought you were going to bring her back, not sit here and enjoy the show while she got drunk." Angela turned and ordered Terry, "Sweety, that's enough. We have to get you home. Leighann, I can't believe you are letting her do this."

"What do you want me to do? She is a grown woman and I can only do so much." Leighann defended herself.

Terry sat with her eyes closed while her friends argued over her, feeling the heat from the alcohol spread through her body. She felt that oh so familiar wave of alcohol induced peace start to float past her eyelids, her signal that she was done. She just didn't want to feel anything right now. She would sleep the rest of the ride home and drift off easily again once she reached the comfort of her bed.

Terry slowly opened her eyes and turned to her companions, smiled slightly and declared, "Ladies, I think I'll need an escort." She slapped $30 on the bar and stood still for a moment to make sure she had her bearings. Leighann and Angela took post on either side of her. Threading their arms through hers, they escorted her back to Angela's

Mercedes where she quickly drifted to sleep for the remainder of the journey home, oblivious to the conversation floating around about her.

When the car pulled up in front of Terry's house, Leighann shook Terry by the shoulder to wake her. But it proved to be a little more difficult than she expected. It had been such a long time since Terry downed that much alcohol at one time. So Angela got out of the car to help guide Terry to her door and up to her room. They slipped her dress from her shoulders and let it fall to the floor. Sitting her between her sheets, they removed the dress from around her ankles and her sandals from her delicate feet in one motion.

Terry rolled into the fluffy thickness of her comforter. It felt so good next to her flushed skin. She tried to open her eyes but the room moved a little more than she could handle and she moaned and slid deeper into the covers.

Thinking Angela wouldn't hear her, Leighann muttered under her breath, "Serves you right." But Angela's look told her she did not approve.

It was just after 4 o'clock but they all felt drained. Angela decided that she would stay and watch Terry for the night. Krystine could not help herself. Before she left to prepare for her flight to LA the next morning, she had to let the others know just how disappointed she was that Terry's drama robbed her of a major photo opportunity. And of course, Leighann had to follow up with telling Krystine just what a jerk she was being. The two clashed regularly but would fight on the front line for each other if necessary.

In college, Leighann made cursing into an art form. And unless Terry was in class or a business setting, she wasn't too far behind her. After Terry made the decision to change her life, Leighann tried hard to respect Terry's wishes that she not curse in her presence. It made it too easy to slip back into old habits. But since Terry was asleep, she took this chance to paint such a vibrant picture, a sailor would blush. When Leighann was through, Krystine simply picked up her keys and walked out, slamming the door behind her.

"Well, I guess I won't be getting a Christmas card this year." Leighann laughed.

"Ya think?" Was all Angela had to say about it.

Leighann went to get the keys to Terry's other car since neither she nor Angela had driven this morning.

"I'm going home to change. Do you want me to stop at your place for anything?"

"No. I have a few things in the guest closet. I should have dinner ready by the time you get back." Angela turned to Leighann, "You are coming back, right?"

"Yes. I will bring the Beamer back as soon as I change." Leighann rolled her eyes and disappeared down the steps to the garage.

Angela started dinner and ran upstairs to change. She checked on Terry and went back down to wait on Leighann to return. They took turns checking on Terry throughout the night but the night was uneventful. It wasn't the whole bottle this time, but Angela would be glad when Terry woke up the next morning. Angela also remembered the last time Terry had way too much to drink.

CHAPTER FOUR
SUNDAY

Sunday morning was on its way to afternoon when Terry finally opened her eyes to the world. Everything seemed so still. But the peace she usually felt on Sunday was not there. Fortunate for her, Angela made her take an aspirin and take in some water in the middle of the night.

Terry sat up slowly just in case her hiatus from alcohol weakened her tolerance level drastically. She slid her back to the headboard and pulled her knees to her chest. Sitting there in disbelief, a new wave of sadness overcame her. She dropped her head to her knees and let the tears flow freely until her sobbing passed.

She had men walk out of her life before, on their own as well as at her command. But never had she experienced such hurt, humiliation, and anger. And twice in less than one week by the same man. Reggie made a fool of her. How in the world could she have been so blind that she could miss all the signs that were now so crystal clear? The more she thought about the things she overlooked, the sicker she felt.

She did not want to face Angela yet but she couldn't stay hidden in her room forever. Just as she threw the covers back she heard her bedroom door open.

"Oh, you're up." Angela stepped back into the hallway to give Terry a moment to grab her robe.

"Are you decent?"

"Yeah." Terry sat on the side of the bed and Angela came over to kneel in front of her and took her hands.

"Are you okay?" Angela asked. Her face was covered in concern while closely watching Terry's mannerisms and motions. She did not know Terry the longest but she was the most protective of her. And she could tell that Terry had been crying again.

"I'll be okay. One day."

"Sooner than you think sweetheart." Angela encouraged her softly with a smile. "Come on. Wash your face and come down and eat. You need something on your stomach."

"Alright. I'll be down in a minute." Terry moved towards the bathroom. "I hope you picked up some.."

"I got your strawberries," Angela cut her off. "And, I threw in a lot of whipped cream. Now," she stood with her hands playfully on her hips, "who's your best friend?"

"Krystine of course!" Terry sniped before she skipped into the bathroom with a squeal. Slamming the door, she blocked the pillow that flew through the air.

Terry sat on the side of her garden bathtub to catch her breath. She took her bible from the book stand and opened it to Psalms 70 and 71. She read slowly, sometimes repeating a line or verse until she felt it sink in. When she finished, she closed her Bible and prayed to God to help her walk through this and to give her peace while she did it.

"Father God, in the name of Jesus, give me strength, guide my footsteps and keep me focused. This situation with Reggie is a huge blow but I know you can see me through this. I know in my heart that you have never left me and you never will. So, I really need you to give me peace. Thank you Lord. Amen." She sat in silence for a moment before she jumped into the shower to try and wash away the rest of yesterday.

CHAPTER FIVE

Leighann was sitting on the couch flipping the TV channels between T. D. Jakes, K. L. Warren and Joseph Prince when Terry finally made her way down the stairs. Propping her feet on the ottoman, Leighann did a little eeny meeny and settled on Pastor Warren to get her word for the week. Terry smiled a bit. Knowing his ministry, Leighann would definitely get a mouthful today. And she needed it. Boy, did she need it. He's usually the one she tuned in to when she missed her own church service and had even begun recording his church's services. He didn't just preach at you, he taught you and even challenged you to check what he taught you. Her study time had changed drastically since she added his lessons to her study time. She had a great foundation where she attended locally. But lately she felt things changing for her spiritually and this ministry was answering a need within her.

Leighann only went to the church building one or two Sundays a month. But it was definitely an improvement over her years of being an E.M.C. member. Easter, Mother's Day and Christmas.

"I see you're getting your poolside praise on." Terry teased Leighann

.

"Without the pool, I am sad to say. The thanks I get for being such a dedicated friend." Leighann responded.

"Um hum. I told you about playing with my Jesus." Terry scolded.

Leighann followed Terry into the kitchen whining all the way.

"Ange', I'm hungry. Are you done yet? Terry is downstairs. Now can we eat?!"

Angela set three plates on the table for them to serve themselves. Terry hit the pancakes first and smothered them in Angela's famous strawberry topping, which she had to sample before she could continue fixing her plate. She sat back in her chair to slowly savor the sweet warmth before she swallowed. When she opened her eyes, Angela was smiling like a proud mother who made her sick child feel better.

"Thank you Angie, I needed that." Terry winked at Leighann before she continued, "It's almost better than sex."

Angela wasn't expecting her spirited comment and almost choked on her turkey bacon. "You must be feeling better."

Leighann chimed in, "Now who's playing with the Lord? You know you are lying."

The ladies' laughter relaxed Terry and she was able to enjoy her breakfast. Terry asked about Krystine and was told that she had called to check on her. She wanted to stop by before her flight but ran out of time.

Terry was only halfway through her stack when Leighann reached for more. She was fit but that woman could eat. Her plate was almost cleared of second helpings before Terry could taste the last bite on her first plate. They were quizzing Angela on her next charity project, the planning of a benefit for the Atlanta Women's Shelter, when the phone rang.

Leighann's guard immediately went up and she grabbed the phone. "Yes? Who's calling?"

She relaxed once she learned it was Terry's assistant Anthony.

"Oh, hold on a moment. It's An-thony." Leighann purred as she handed the phone to Terry.

"Hey, what's up?" Terry tried so hard to conceal her laughter. Anthony hated when Leighann talked to him like Eartha Kitt.

Angela and Leighann took this break in their conversation to get more juice from the refrigerator.

Suddenly, Terry's fork hit her plate and Angela nearly dropped the juice to the floor. They turned to find Terry with her head in her hand.

Leighann made it to her side first. "What happened? Do I need to get my purse?"

Terry held up her hand to quiet her friends so she could hear what Anthony was saying.

"But Anthony, what happened? The messenger picked up the contract from me before the cops even had a chance to question me at the accident scene. So I know it was there on time and in Tadashi's hand. I was talking to him when it was put there. All he had to do was sign it. He said he was sending it back to the office, by messenger, Friday afternoon."

Anthony voice was filled with panic. "Well, it did not arrive by five. So I called his assistant Karen. She told me he was still looking through it with legal but had instructed her to get their messenger ready. Kayla was going to wait for it to arrive and when I didn't hear from her I assumed everything went as planned."

"Obviously you forgot what assuming does." Terry was trying to stay calm but was failing. "Sorry. So, where is the contract now?"

"With Tadashi." That took Terry's breath away.

"Anthony. Tadashi left for Tokyo. Yesterday!"

"That's not all." Anthony took a deep breath and Terry's stomach dropped lower along with her head. "Somehow, Cameron Robertson talked his way onto Tadashi's plane."

"Oh, hell!" Terry slid her plate away and lowered her head to the table. That was the last thing she needed. Cameron went after every job and every account she ever worked on. Rivals since grad school, he was like a bloodhound. Angela tried to console her but Terry just pushed her away.

"I don't believe this. We have to get to Tadashi." Now Terry's whispered plea held a touch of panic.

"I already tried. Karen said he makes one call when he lands and then he is out of contact for at least 24 hours. Unless his building is on fire, he is unreachable."

Terry sat silent so long that Anthony thought she hung up.

"Terry? Terry, you there?"

"Yeah. Just get through to him when you can. I, I can't do this right now." Terry dropped the phone to the table and rose from her chair.

Angela grabbed the phone and told Anthony she'd call him later and hung up so she could catch Terry.

"Terry." She kept walking.

"Terry! Stop!" Leighann ordered.

Terry stood there with her head lowered and eyes closed.

Angela asked, "Where are you going?"

Terry didn't want to talk anymore. She let out a deep sigh before she answered softly, "Upstairs."

"And?" When she didn't answer Leighann became nervous and almost yelled. "And then what?"

Terry looked up at her friends and opened her mouth but nothing came out at first.

"I don't know." She was fighting to hold back her tears. "I don't know. I just want to go back to bed." And without another word, she turned and walked upstairs to her room and quietly closed the door.

Angela cracked open her door just as Terry was pulling the comforter around her neck. Angela watched her lie there for a moment in silence before she turned her face into her pillow and wept. She wanted to run to Terry's side but she had no idea of what to say or do. So she closed the door softly and slid to the floor and sat there praying for her best friend. Angela was never at a loss for words or scriptures but right now she only had tears and prayers for her friend. "Hear our heart's cry, Lord."

Leighann waited as long as she could before she crept up the stairs to find Angela sitting in front of the bedroom door. She heard Angela's whispers and turned to go back downstairs. She did not want to interrupt the prayers being sent up.

Three hours later, the phone rang only once before Leighann grabbed it.

"Yes?"

"Terry?" It was Anthony. "Sweetheart, are you alright?"

"It's Leighann. And no, she is not alright. Ant, what the hell is going on?"

Anthony told her what happened. They were both surprised that Terry had not informed her friends of just how important this deal was for her team.

Normally very talkative, Leighann sat quietly and listened intently so she could give Angela a complete report of the conversation.

The ladies were on Terry's very short list of approved confidantes so Anthony felt safe sharing with Leighann.

When he reached the end of his tale, Anthony asked Leighann to call him whenever Terry awoke, no matter the time. He wanted to talk once more if possible before they returned to work the next day. There would be a lot of explaining to do and he wanted to be well prepared to face Mr. Clayton.

CHAPTER SIX

Terry didn't open her eyes again until after seven and she noticed her bedroom door was only half closed. Even though the house was quiet, she knew she wasn't alone.

Angela, who ended up falling asleep outside her door for over an hour earlier that afternoon, was now sitting with Leighann and Krystine, who changed her flight to be there for her friend. They were watching someone's home get demolished to rebuild their lives. Angela wished that somehow she could do the same for her friend.

Since Terry did not get to finish her brunch, and by now she was starving. "Father, I am going to try and get up again. Can I please have something to eat without any drama?"

Terry slid from underneath her comforter to prepare to face her girls. Looking at her reflection in the dresser mirror, she encouraged herself. "We're going to try this again. Remember, through all of this, God has your back. You may not understand why these things are happening, but you do know that God has never let you down. A solution is close by. A positive end to this trial is near. Let patience have her perfect work. Remember James 1:1-5. Thank you Lord for getting me through this."

Feeling a little better and more at peace, Terry made her way down to the kitchen. Her friends didn't hear her come down the stairs and Krystine jumped up from her chair when she heard the refrigerator door close.

"Terry! Babe are you alright?" Krystine made a beeline to the kitchen with Leighann and Angela close on her heels.

"I'm okay Krys. It's been a bumpy few days but I am still in one piece. And starving."

"Well then, let's eat!" Leighann grabbed a cold drumstick off Terry's plate and bit into it. "I just realized that I haven't eaten in hours."

With that, everyone else fell into rhythm with her and set out to eat their way through the evening. Although she was quite hungry, her desire to eat left pretty quickly once she stopped the hunger pains with a few bites.

They talked and joked around until Terry noticed it was after ten.

"Ladies, I have to be in the office early tomorrow to handle this situation with Anthony. You know he will be waiting."

"Yeess. An-thony will be waiting." Leighann added her Eartha Kitt impression making them burst into laughter. "He said to give him a call, no matter the time."

"He'll be fine. I'll see him in the morning." Terry waived off Anthony's request.

Terry bid her friends a good night and locked up for the evening. The girls helped her clean up so all that was left to do was to go to sleep. She was amazed that she still could after all the hours she spent beneath the covers that day. She wanted to be well rested, so she put on soft worship music to sleep to and kept her mind focused on positive thoughts and prayers. Just before she fell asleep she whispered, "I am well skilled, highly favored and covered by the grace of God. I know you'll show me which way to go. So, I am going to rest now, in you Lord. This hasn't been easy and I thank you for keeping me while I'm going through this. Even when I was the one who made the unwise choices. Good night and I'll see you in the morning as we work this thing out. Amen."

CHAPTER SEVEN
MONDAY

Monday morning, Terry rose from bed with a new attitude. She laid everything down before God last night as she prayed while getting into bed. Today would be a new day. She had entirely too much to do to dwell on the drama of the last week.

At six thirty, Terry walked into her office to find Anthony leaning over her desk writing her a note.

"Ah hem," she cleared her throat.

"And you are late." Anthony finished writing his note and stuck it on her monitor. "I've been here for an hour already and you give me attitude."

"Dude, I am attitude. Deal with it." Terry said with a wink and moved behind her desk.

"Well, all right then. Let's get busy and fix this mess we're in."

For the next two hours they focused on finalizing their second highest priority project. Although there were only a few minor changes that needed to be made, it took a great deal of time to make sure all of the figures were within budget.

If they received a call from Tadashi's people, his contract could be saved. But they could not wait for that to happen. It helped that they always had several projects running at the same time. They would not be empty handed when Mr. Clayton called on them to deliver.

Shortly after nine, they took a break to grab something to eat. When they walked back into Terry's office her assistant Kayla interrupted their conversation. "Mr. Clayton called a meeting."

Terry and Anthony stopped in their tracks and looked at each other.

"Well?" Anthony raised his head high and told her, "The moment of truth has arrived."

A confident smile appeared on Terry's face. "We're covered." She turned back to her assistant, "Alright Kayla, when and where?"

"10 a.m. in the conference room."

"The conference room?" Terry quizzed Anthony. "Then it can't be what we think." She turned back to Kayla, "What's the story?"

Kayla was the ultimate news source. She knew what their CEO was having for dinner before he did. But this time, she was no help.

"I don't know. And believe me, I asked the right people and they gave up nothing. Sorry, I can't help you."

"That's alright. Anthony let's get ready." They went into her office and prepared for the meeting.

When they emerged shortly before ten, they had on their game faces. Terry was confident that if they had to give a report, what they had would still impress Mr. Clayton.

The conference room was half full when Terry and Anthony arrived. They moved to occupy the two seats at the far end of the table. But Anthony made sure he left the seat at the very end for her. If Clayton took the seat at the head of the table, he most certainly did not want to be the face looking back at him.

Terry had her hand on the back of the seat when Anthony plopped down and gave her the "sorry" look.

"That's real funny Anthony. You will pay for this." She whispered in his ear as she walked past him to the last available seat at the table.

"I simply made an executive decision. I want you to be in the appropriate position to adequately explain our current status." Anthony replied with mock sincerity and a mischievous glint in his eyes.

Terry firmly sat her coffee cup on the table and slowly lowered herself to her seat while making a promise. "And I shall see to it that your dedication is adequately rewarded to my complete satisfact..." Terry lost her breath and felt a chill run through her body. She would have missed her chair if Anthony wasn't pushing it in. Mr. Clayton's entrance caught her eye, but his companion made her world spin.

"Terry?" When she didn't respond, Anthony slid his chair closer and pushed her arm with his. "Terry?"

"What?" She barely whispered turning to Anthony.

"What happened? You almost missed your chair."

Terry looked away. Careful to appear calm, she grabbed her coffee and slowly lifted the cup to her lips.

Looking at the front of the room over the rim of her mug, she couldn't believe her eyes. Her past was standing in front of her.

Michael Jacobs stood next to Mr. Clayton, smiling like he didn't have a care in the world or care that he had just put hers in a tailspin. He was six foot two with soft brown hair and his tan reflected his days in the California sun. Michael's eyes were a deep brown. But they would change with his mood and emotions. They were a chestnut, almost hazel brown when he was relaxed. She knew from intimate experience that he was either anxious or excited. Before she knew it, her mind flashed to the first time he kissed her. She remembered his eyes were almost the same color. Her body immediately responded to the memory, sending a wave of emotion through her that she hadn't felt in years. But then, just as suddenly, her chest and stomach began to ache and she had to fight to clear her mind of the hurt he caused her the very last time their lips met. It was the last time she saw him.

She fought too hard five years ago to overcome the hurt, depression, anger and outburst of rage, to allow her heart to break all over again just from the sight of him. "I won't go back to that place," she thought to herself. She took a deep breath and focused on Mr. Clayton's voice as he called the meeting to order.

Anthony, sensing the change in her demeanor, became all business. He quickly zeroed in and began to take in all the details of his surroundings. Especially Terry.

"Good Morning everyone. Let's get started." Everyone turned their attention forward, giving her temporary relief from Anthony's curious stare.

"I know you all are working very hard so I will not prolong my announcement. I'll get straight to the point. We all know that Harvey Langston has moved on to explore other career options, leaving open the position of Senior Manager – Media." Terry took another slow steadying breath. Everyone was expecting her to be placed in that position, but with Michael Jacobs standing in the room during the announcement, they all knew that was not to be. She knew all eyes would turn to gauge her reactions. And she was determined to keep her face steady and unaffected. Terry would not allow anyone to see just how shaken and surprised she was.

"I want to introduce to you Michael Jacobs. He was the Director of Advertising for a major firm in Los Angeles for the last three years. He is also a two time CLIO Award winner and our new Senior Manager - Media." The room erupted in applause as was expected. But the looks on the faces of Terry's co-workers ranged from confusion to dutiful acceptance.

Terry thought to herself, "Clio Award? Hmmp. I have four of them. Why is this man, of all people, getting my job?"

Mr. Clayton continued once the room settled. "We are fortunate to have Michael joining us. I want you to welcome him and assist him in any way he needs to get up to speed on your current projects. Michael, I present to you your new team."

Michael stepped forward to take over the meeting. Michael's voice sent a shock through Terry's system. It had been such a long time since she had heard his deep velvet British accent, but it washed over her like it was yesterday.

"Good morning everyone. It is a pleasure to be here with you and to be a part of such an awesome team. Your reputation precedes you."

She tried hard to focus on his words but her mind kept presenting images of him smiling, laughing, and holding her close to him. As soon as she would gather her thoughts from one emotional rewind to focus on what he was saying, something else about him would set her mind on another journey through her former life. His hands, his smiling lips, the way his suit outlined his very fit and matured frame.

For those few minutes, Terry was definitely not in control of her own body. Their former relationship was a very passionate one. Her flashes of memory were unexpected. And she was not mentally prepared to guard against the intense sensations that flowed at will through her body. That is, until the memory of their last kiss popped into her head again. And suddenly, she was very focused on the man standing before her.

Terry lowered her eyes to her coffee cup and breathed deeply. The last day they saw each other changed her life, utterly shaking her to her core. Although it only took seconds for that day to play back in her mind, every little detail seemed as fresh as if it were happening right then. But a tremor began in the pit of her stomach when she heard Michael's next words.

"There is, however, one thing that I would like to accomplish quickly. I would like to take some time to sit down with each of you so that I can get a clearer picture of what your goals are and where we are on your current and planned projects. I think the time we spend will also help you to become a little more familiar with who I am and what I have to offer our team."

Terry's heart began to pound so loud in her ears, she felt like everyone would hear it.

"Hmm, our team alright," Anthony whispered under his breath.

"Quiet," Terry whispered back, nudging his foot.

Michael continued, "I don't want to take up too much of your time. Maybe fifteen to thirty minutes sometime over the next week or so."

Michael's eyes seemed to direct his next words in Terry's direction. "I know how busy you are and I do respect your time." He looked away then, before his stare became obvious. "With that said, I look forward to speaking with each of you. Thank you for the warm welcome and hospitality. Mr. Clayton?"

"Thank you Michael. I know he'll be a perfect fit for our organization.

Everyone, check your calendars and call his assistant Amy to set a time for your conference." Mr. Clayton made a point of making eye contact with several key individuals in the room before concluding the meeting. This signal was to make sure they understood no excuses would be tolerated.

"Thank you all for coming. Have a good morning."

Everyone rose and headed to the front of the room. Terry thanked God that there were too many people around Michael for her to make physical contact. Instead, when they made eye contact, she nodded, and said "Welcome" loud enough for those standing near to hear, and then moved to leave the room. She stopped to speak briefly to Roger and Tasha, just to make sure her exit didn't appear too hasty.

As she exited the room, Kayla tried to hand her a message. But all Terry could think of was getting as far away as she could so she could crack the lid on her emotions. She was about to explode and all she was able to get out was, "Hold on to it. Be back in 15."

She turned and walked away, heading for the stairwell. Terry climbed from the 8th floor to the empty tenth floor where they had yet to complete renovations. She headed to the ladies restroom. Closing the door to the end stall, she leaned against the wall as if she were being frisked. She pressed hard against the wall, trying to make her arms and stomach stop shaking. She was definitely in the right place. Before she knew it, she was bent over giving up her breakfast. She grabbed a wad of tissue to wipe her mouth. This cannot be happening.

"Dear Lord!? Daddy? Father! Please, please tell me. What on earth is happening? I can't do this. This man wants to sit and talk like we've never met. Is he serious? Lord, you have got to get me out of this!" Yelling that last plea, Terry heard Angela's calm voice in her mind telling her that God would not put more on her than she could bear. "Angela get out of my head! I need help." She softly propped her head against the wall and fought the tears that she felt coming.

Terry turned and leaned her back against the cool wall for several minutes. She was trying to get up the nerve to walk out of the bathroom and face Anthony when she returned to her office. She knew he would be there waiting to decipher what just went down.

Both the meeting itself and her overall reaction. Terry shared many things with him over the years since they began working together and became friends, but Michael Jacobs was not one of them. This would for certain be on his list of things to talk about.

"Damn, damn, damn!" Her emotions were once again trying to get out of control. They were being shaken in such a strange way. At least the last time she saw Michael, she knew what to feel. Anger.

CHAPTER EIGHT
FLASHBACK: FIVE YEARS AGO

"M.J. I'm home." Terry walked into the condo she shared with Michael Jacobs. She dubbed him M.J. after their first official date to a costume party. She was Tina Turner but he would not tell her what he was wearing. About a week prior, after his fourth beer, he confided that he had an extensive Michael Jackson collection at his parent's home in England. But she was still so very surprised when she opened her front door to greet him, that she burst out in laughter. There stood before her a caucasian Michael Jackson with a British accent. She laughed so much that night that she stopped thinking so much about the color of his skin. All she saw was that beautiful smile beneath his captivating hazel brown eyes. The low timbre of his voice coupled with his accent didn't hurt either. A year later, here they were living together, deeply in love and looking forward to what would come next.

Hanging up her jacket in the front hall closet, she called out for him again with excitement in her voice, "Hey, babe? Are you home?"

Terry walked into the living room and saw Michael sitting on the couch. "Didn't you hear me calling you? Look, Angela and Carl have invited us to dinner at the Mayor's reception tomorrow. I tell you, it really pays to have friends in high places." She stopped talking and stood still in the middle of the room. Something wasn't right. The air in the room felt heavy and her stomach did another flip. She had been having this feeling in her stomach for the last few days and thought that she might be pregnant. She and Michael had spoken often of a family. Although she hadn't formally discussed it with him yet, she had decided just this month not to continue her birth control and would wait to see what happened. It would be a wonderful surprise for Michael. He would be a great dad. But she was disappointed this morning when the test she bought on the way to work gave her a negative result. "Well, there's always tonight," she smiled and winked at her reflection in the bathroom mirror. "After all, making the baby is half the fun," she declared as she turned away to go back her desk.

But right now, that feeling was making her very uneasy. And Michael's demeanor didn't help at all.

"M.J.?" His head sank deeper into his hands and Terry no longer felt uneasy. She felt downright ill. When she spoke again, her words were almost a whisper. It was suddenly hard to breathe. "Michael? Honey what's wrong?"

"I've been trying to figure out how to tell you." Michael said after a long pause. He rose from where he was sitting at the far end of the couch, visibly struggling to find words.

Confused, Terry questioned, "Tell me what? Michael, what's going on?" Her stomach did another flip and she swallowed hard.

He took a step her way but she retreated with a raised hand to stop him. This couldn't be good and she wanted to keep a clear head.

"Tell me what?" She didn't take her eyes away from his face. She wanted the truth. All of it. He couldn't look at her and turned away.

"I have to leave town." Michael said softly and then paused to wait for her next question. But it never came. Terry didn't speak but kept her eyes on him, giving him nothing to grab on to. Whatever it was, it was big. And he had to explain this on his own.

He had never seen Terry really upset and he didn't know what to expect as she stood there silently watching him.

"I have to return to England." Terry's eyes narrowed in suspicion. He had gone home before, but there was never an air of tension surrounding his trip like there was now. Her anger management training was slowly losing its grip. And her calm was shaking. But she wanted to hear everything before she let her emotions take over. Something was not right. And she hated the waiting game when it came to spilling secrets.

"Michael." That was her warning. When he did not respond, it pissed her off and she let her anger surface.

"Tell Me!" she commanded.

"There is someone else," came out in a whisper.

Terry's chest felt like it was about to burst and suddenly she couldn't breath.

With tears of anger filling her eyes, she pushed her next words out. "What? What do you mean someone else?" He let the silence linger again. With her fists balled up at her sides, she demanded of him, "Tell me damn it!"

Michael was having a very hard time. But at this point, Terry didn't really care how he felt. He would give her the whole truth and then he would pay.

"It's been planned for years. In three months our families expect..," he blurted, trying to explain quickly but his voice failed at the sight of Terry's disbelief. "I mean, it's just that... This is coming out all wrong." He turned away and started pacing back and forth until Terry's words stopped him.

"Fourteen months?" Terry couldn't believe what she was hearing. She stood there shaking her head in disbelief. "For over a year you hid this from me. Asking me if I loved you and, and to be with you. Talking about family and, and children. Oh God, children! And now you decide to let me in on your little secret because you have no choice. You, are a liar!" She was screaming but the time she was finished.

"I'm sorry, I'm so sorry."

"You're sorry?! You're damn right you're sorry!" She felt her body trembling and she wanted to hit him with all the power she could muster. "I am such an idiot! I trusted you. How could you lie like this? What kind of man are you?!"

If Terry wasn't so angry, she could've had compassion for how helpless he looked. He started pacing the floor again. "I didn't mean to fall in love," he started and then changed gears at Terry's reaction to his hurtful words. "I mean, I wasn't supposed to stay here. Grad school and then back to London. That was the plan That's how it was supposed to be." He stopped to face her again. "But, then I met you. And I didn't want to be anywhere else. I thought I could change things at home and make my life here. With you. But they won't let me."

"They? You're a grown ass man. You make your own choices." Terry turned to walk into the kitchen. "I'm tired of hearing you talk."

"Terry, please understand."

"Understand? Understand what, you coward?" She mocked his accent knowing he didn't like her to do that when she was angry. "You coming into my life and lying to me about what I had to look forward to with you? Lying to me about who you are and stealing time out of my life? Making me want things, a future, a family? You ass! I thought I was pregnant!"

Michael's mouth dropped opened. "What? You thought?"

"Yeah, thought. I've had this weird feeling in the pit of my stomach for days and I thought it might be a baby. Instead, it turns out that my intuition has been trying warn me about the snake sleeping under my own covers." Terry turned to walk away again. "Get out before I lose it! Go back to your mum. I don't ever want to see your face again."

Michael followed her and reached for her arm to stop her. He spun her around so fast she found her back up against the wall with him standing only a hair's breadth from pressing up against her. This time, she didn't see fear in his eyes. And she wanted what she saw. She felt herself momentarily drawn to the Michael she knew before today.

"Our child?" Michael looked down her body, causing a shiver to run through her. Their desire ran deep. And as angry as she was right now, she couldn't ignore those feelings. It had been that way from the very first time they kissed. It was so natural to be close to him, in every way. So when his demeanor and focus changed, she shifted right along with him.

"I told you no." She whispered fighting back her tears again.

Before she could move away, Michael wrapped his arms around her and pulled her tightly to his chest. "Oh baby," he whispered in her ear. A soft cry escaped from her throat and she pressed deeper into his embrace. She hadn't let herself feel the full extent of her disappointment in the negative test results. She had decided that there was no need to be upset because they had plenty of time to work on the family they talked so much about. Their discussions about the future were deep and exhilarating. Although they did not always agree on every detail, they still connected on every level in some way. Sometimes it astounded her how a disagreement between them could end up with them making love for hours, sometimes never parting in the spaces where they slept wrapped together. They fit together so well. That's why when he slid lips across hers, instinctively she responded by parting hers further, allowing her body to respond to the excitement his mouth was creating. He always took his time with her. His hands traveled slowly down her back to her firm backside. She loved the sensations Michael created in her body when he touched her. She gasped when he cupped her bottom and pulled her hips tight against his. Her arousal now matching the obvious state of his as he pressed her body against the wall. Her emotions were everywhere and she wasn't prepared to resist him. Being with him felt so right and she wanted him to stay in her arms.

But Terry heard her mind screaming, "Stay? He's not staying!" Immediately her eyes flew open and her surroundings registered. She felt a panic rising from the midst of all the intense sexual energy flowing through her body.

Her mind flashed an image of another woman standing in her place in his embrace. Terry's angry suddenly returned in full force. Before she knew it, she caught him off guard and pushed him so hard he hit the opposite wall.

Dazed, in a mix of surprise and passion, Michael stood up and reached out for her. But his time, when he moved towards her, her self preservation instincts took over. "NO!" She yelled. "You won't make a fool of me again!" She swung her right fist as hard as she could at his midsection. Taken by surprise again, he fell to the floor. And this time he didn't jump back up.

Terry quickly turned and went into the kitchen and grabbed a bottle of Tequila from the cabinet. She didn't want to feel anything right now. And she knew that Tequila would do the trick.

When she came out of the kitchen, Michael was slowly rising from the floor, holding his ribs with his face twisted in pain.

"Serves you right. Get the hell out of my life. And don't you ever come back. Forget where I live and my name. As a matter of fact, you can forget I ever existed."

"Terry, wait."

"Whatever man, get the hell out before I call the cops."

Terry turned her back on him and walked away forever. When she was done, she was done.

She went to her room where she slammed and locked the door. Sitting on the side of her bed, she put the tequila bottle to her lips and swallowed as much as she could before the burn made her choke. With her eyes closed, she sat in silence listening to hear her front door close. She didn't drink liquor often and her head quickly began to spin pretty quickly. Still feeling the pain in her chest, she raised the bottle and swallowed again. "I don't want to feel anything right now." she proclaimed through her tears.

She heard Michael walk up to her bedroom door. But he only stood there. For a full minute she fought to sit still and upright, trying not to make a sound, before he gave up and walked away. When Terry heard her front door close, she labeled him "coward" for the second time before she drank from the bottle again. She never drank on an empty stomach. The alcohol was taking effect quicker than she'd ever experienced. But still chasing relief from her pain, she didn't stop drinking.

When the phone rang, she knocked the receiver to the floor trying to answer it. With tears running down her face, she slid to her knees. She felt for the phone while leaning her head against the side of the bed.

She heard Angela's voice calling her name before the phone reached her ear.

"What?" Although in her mind she had yelled out the word, it was only a whisper.

"Terry?

"What Ang?" Terry slurred.

They spoke only a half hour ago and Angela could tell that something was wrong.

"Are you alright? What's going on?" Angela asked, her senses on high alert.

"No. I am not alright. That bum ..." Terry started to cry.

Her heart beginning to beat a mile a minute, Angela grabbed her keys, transferred the call from her office to her cell phone and headed to her car. She could make it to Terry's in 10 minutes or less. "Tell me what happened," she ordered into her cellphone. "Got an emergency." Angela whispered to her secretary as she whisked by not looking back.

"He left me Angie." Terry put the Tequila bottle to her lips again until it was almost gone. Although the alcohol had dulled her senses to the point where she barely felt the burn, she still coughed from the attack on her throat.

Angela started to panic when she heard the phone drop again. "Terry? Terry?!" she called into the phone while she paced on the elevator ride to the ground floor. "Oh Lord. Terry, please answer me!" She felt only a moment of relief when she heard Terry coughing.

"Angie?"

"Yes baby, I'm on the way." Angela tried to keep her voice calm. She slid into her car and pulled out of the office building's garage.

Terry had never taken in so much alcohol so quickly. She didn't feel the pain in her chest anymore but her stomach was beginning to rebel. "Angie?"

"Terry, how much did you drink?" Angela asked cautiously.

"Um, don't know. Bottle. I.." Terry tried to hold on to her consciousness but she was fading quickly. The room was spinning way too fast. In her mind, Terry was telling Angela everything but only bits and pieces made it past her lips until she couldn't stay upright anymore. "I.. help...," was all she got out before she dropped the phone for the last time and passed out on the floor.

Angela couldn't bring herself to hang up so she grabbed her work cell phone and dialed 911 to summon an ambulance to Terry's rescue. She would make it there before they would. But she wasn't sure what she would find when she arrived. This last mile seemed to take forever. And Angela ran every red light she encountered, ignoring the horns blasting at her.

The sirens could be heard as Angela ran to Terry's front door and used the key she had for emergencies. She left the door wide open and frantically looked through the apartment until she came to the locked bedroom door. She banged on the door yelling out Terry's name. When she didn't get an answer, she went into a full panic and kicked the door with all her might until it flew open.
 Angela's heart plunged further into her stomach at the sight of Terry on the floor. She fell to the floor next to Terry and shook her, calling her name. She had just pulled Terry onto her back and positioned herself above her to listen for signs of breathing when the EMT's arrived. They quickly moved Angela out of the way to assess Terry's status. Angela told them all she knew and handed over the near empty tequila bottle while they checked Terry's vitals and prepared her for transport. Terry was breathing, but very faintly. They put an oxygen mask over her mouth and nose and put her limp body on the stretcher. Angela grabbed Terry's purse and jumped into the ambulance behind the stretcher.

At the hospital, Angela refused to leave Terry's side. The only thing that kept her from the room was a very stern nurse that made her understand that she could become a distraction to the doctors. Not willing to do anything that would hamper Terry's treatment, she paced the floor. Quietly keeping her eyes on the hospital room door.

Around midnight, Terry came to, calling Angela's name. She only meant to rest her head on the bed next to Terry, but had fallen into a deep sleep. She was able to relax a bit once the doctor assured her that Terry would be ok. She jumped up when Terry's voice registered through her troubled dream, "I'm right here sweetheart." Terry had tears in her eyes and Angela's heart felt like it was breaking. She buzzed for the nurse and stood by until she completed her evaluation and left the room.

Angela perched herself gently on the bed beside Terry and took her hand. "Terry, can you talk about what happened? I need to know why you drank so much."

When Terry opened her mouth to speak, nothing came out. Angela fought to remain calm. Frustrated by her silence, she gently urged Terry to open up. "Terry, you had alcohol poisoning. I need you to tell me what happened. Now, sweetheart."

With tears streaming down her face, Terry tried again. Talking through her sobs, she told Angela what happened with Michael.

Angela became angrier the more Terry told her. She didn't want to make matters worse, so she kept silent until after Terry finished. Then she pulled Terry into her arms and held her close to her heart. Only negative thoughts of Michael were surfacing. So she kept her lips tightly closed for fear that she would send Terry into another fit of tears.

They sat together quietly for a while until the nurse returned to check Terry's vitals again.

Terry was able to leave the hospital the next day, but not Angela's watchful care. She practically moved Terry into her home for the next week and made her rest. Fortunately, Angela had the connections to put Terry on a "special assignment" with the city so that she would not lose her job.

Angela worked half days for the next week. They talked as much or as little as Terry wanted. She was able to release her tears and anger and talk through the beginning of her healing.

By the time Terry went back to work, she was able to keep her emotions in check to get through the day. Her apartment was different without Michael. But there was nothing she could do about it. Nothing she wanted to do about it. Except get over it. "Thank God I didn't get pregnant. I won't make that mistake again."

Her first morning back to work came with a vengeance. Filled with new resolve and purpose, she hit the gym before work. She filled every minute of her day with anything that kept her busy. She found solace in her activity and kept busy until bedtime. She was sitting in bed reading papers she'd brought home from work when she realized just how much she had accomplished that day. To her, that meant she was okay. "No need to look back," she declared. "May as well get some rest. I have the world to conquer tomorrow!" she spoke out loud.

From that day forward, Terry was on a new mission to make her mark in the public relations world. Michael, who? No matter what it took, she was taking her life back. And he would not matter in her future.

CHAPTER NINE
MONDAY

Terry got her mind focused and ready to finish out her day. Mr. Clayton's bombshell cannot and will not stop her from reaching today's goal. She emerged from the elevator on her floor with her cell phone plastered to her ear. Before she left the restroom on the 10th floor, she checked her clothes and her attitude and put on her game face. "Alright, time to conquer," she declared to herself. She walked up to the 12th floor which contained their archives and storage area. Pulling out one of her older sample files, she headed back to her office with another idea for the account she was working on earlier that morning.

"That would be lovely Shawna. I'll wait for your call. As long as it's before 2pm today." Terry laughingly demanded. She appeared relaxed and confident. She found a friend in Shawna McQueen when they had to form a partnership to close on a major international deal three years ago. That lead to two other large collaborations, one of which won them an award.

She was hanging up when she walked into her office. Anthony was standing by the window looking through a file. "Hey, where did you go? You know we need to talk about the new team member," he said making the quotation marks in the air emphasizing the last two words.

"Anthony, look. I don't know where this Mr. Jacobs thing came from but I do know I have a great idea for this account." She pulled out the samples folder she brought from upstairs and proceeded to explain her brainstorm.

Anthony gave her a look that very plainly told her that he was not going to let the object of today's meeting fade from the list of topics for discussion. But Terry kept going and eventually pulled his attention to the two samples that she intended to adjust and incorporate into their presentation.

When she was finished, Anthony threw out every question he could think of to shoot the additions down. But Terry had an answer for everything he could think of.

"Well, looks like we have another winner!" Anthony raised his hand for a high-five. "You are a genius at this. I don't know why Clayton brought that Jacobs guy in here to do what is supposed to be your job."

"Don't have the time to dwell on that right now." Terry stopped Anthony's coming tirade cold in its tracks. "I want to have this ready for the client first thing tomorrow morning. I just need to stop by Creative and then I believe we will be finished." Terry stood there with a smile on her face and her arms crossed in satisfaction looking great in her new-found confidence. But then the change in Anthony's face made her spin around to see what he was looking at. Immediately her smile disappeared and for a moment she had no words. But only for a moment. Michael was standing just outside her office door talking with Kayla. "I will not let him see me as weak," she thought to herself. She turned back and walked to her desk, taking the opportunity to also avoid Anthony's observation while she gathered her thoughts.

Anthony spoke first. "Looks like we'll have to make time. You good?"

Terry nodded and continued to prepare her file for the next day's call to their client. "I'm good." They both turned to the door at Michael's knock.

"Good morning again. I hope I am not interrupting anything," Michael said as he entered Terry's office.

"No. We were just reaching a stopping point. Please, have a seat. I didn't know we were already on your schedule." Terry motioned to the empty seat in front of her desk.

"Thank you. I was finishing next door and thought I'd check with Kayla since the two you were already here together. If you don't mind, I won't take too much of your time. How are you?" The question itself was much more innocent than the look in his eyes. Terry sat up a little straighter and quickly looked away.

"I'm fine. Things are well here." Terry decided to make sure she stopped Anthony from leaving her alone. "Anthony and I are working wonders, as usual." She looked over at Anthony and smiled sweetly.

Anthony, who was standing behind Michael, looked back at her like she had lost her mind, his eye screaming "What the hell are you doing? Tell him to get out!" He quickly plastered a serene look on his face as Michael turned to look in his direction.

"I can't take much of the credit," Anthony shrugged. "Simply put, Terry's brilliant."

Michael chuckled and they joined in. That brief moment broke Terry's tension and she relaxed a bit.

"Alright Anthony, enough of the love fest. Mr. Jacobs is not here to find out how much we like each other." Terry turned her attention to Michael. "So, Mr. Jacobs, what would you like to know?"

"Please, call me Michael." Terry's deceptively welcoming demeanor gave him the ok to loosen up. He relaxed in his chair and rested one foot on his opposite knee, making his presence seem even larger. Terry sat further back in her seat behind her desk and crossed her legs at the knee. Maybe she could focus all of her tension there and keep her upper body visibly calm and relaxed.

Michael continued, looking over at Anthony and then back to Terry. "I am very excited to be here. This firm has made such a mark in PR, it is a major accomplishment to have been chosen to be here. So, I truly want to make sure that my transition into this community goes smoothly. Please understand that I am not here to take over, but to be a part of your continued success." Looking between the two of them he continued. "I also recognize that your partnership here in this room is a major reason why this firm has reached its current level of international demand. In fact, your last two campaigns bordered on genius. Guidance is not what you need. It's support. So, please, use me as a resource as much or as little as you need."

She may not have seen this man in over 5 years, but she knew him well enough to recognize his sincerity. Her threat level meter just went down a notch.

"Would either of you have any questions for me?"

"Actually, I do." Anthony spoke first. "Your reputation also precedes you. And, if I may say so, you're sort of a golden boy wherever you go." He paused to let his words sink in. When Michael's demeanor didn't budge, he went on. "I'm taking in all that you just shared with us. But what I'd like to know is how hands on do you plan to be with this," Anthony motioned his hand to include Terry, "partnership that's bordering on genius?"

Terry sat forward in her seat at Anthony's bluntness. "Anthony, I don't think.."

"It's alright Terry," Michael interrupted. "I understand completely where Anthony is coming from." He turned back to address Anthony, lowering his foot to the floor and leaning forward in his chair. "You have a very well oiled machine working here. And frankly, you don't want anyone coming in to make adjustments that you do not need, and that could actually disrupt your workflow. And you certainly don't need anyone coming in trying to take over. Listen, I am not here to make life difficult or to make my name great. I know who I am and I know my worth. I don't have to prove anything to anyone. Like everyone here, I want to be a part of greatness wherever I choose to go. And to be honest, it was time to make a change. It was a great company but I wasn't growing anymore where I was. I searched around and I found you." Michael's eyes locked with Terry's and all of a sudden her heart began to race again.

The silence in the room lingered a moment too long and a slight frown appeared on Anthony's face. Just then, Terry broke her gaze with Michael. Catching Anthony's curious look, she wished she could make him disappear. She would disappear herself if she could.

"Well, um, I'm sure things will work out just fine." Terry quickly stood up behind her desk and clasped her hands in front of her. This usually signaled to a guest, "Thank you for coming. Now the meeting is over and you may leave." However, Michael remained seated and so did Anthony for that matter. Not ready to let either of them off the hook just yet, Anthony decided to dig a little further.

"There's one other thing I'd still like to know. Since we're being so honest here." Michael turned his full attention to him and Terry took that opportunity to walk out of his eyes reach to compose herself, shuffling for nothing in particular through the stack of papers on her credenza.

"Go on," Michael said. Accepting Anthony's challenging tone.

"What exactly were you looking for that made you choose to seek a spot in this firm." Pausing a moment, he added, "Specifically."

Not one to be outdone, Michael slowly smiled and rose from his seat to look from Terry leaning against her credenza with a disapproving frown on her face to Anthony's challenging stare. He moved to stand behind his chair and leaned against it's back. He made direct eye contact with Anthony before responding.

"Why Anthony, what are you referring to? Specifically?" Michael asked with more than a little sarcasm.

Anthony also rose to the occasion. Standing to his full six foot two inch height, he took a step towards Michael's chair and place his hands on his waist. And with narrowed eyes, allowed his voice to reach its deepest timbre.

"If you are looking for a professional conquest, Terry Ellis is not the one. Hear me very clearly. I take my position in her life very seriously. And she has rightfully earned everything she has accomplished."

Standing from his leaning position, Michael crossed his arms across his broad chest. "I can respect your protective position. But I am not here to conquer her professionally."

Anthony immediately responded before Michael could continue.

"And personally. I also pull no punches when it comes to her well-being. Personally."

Terry gasped at Anthony's blunt proclamation. She felt her face, and most of her body for that matter, begin to flush. "Oh no! Anthony, you did not just do that." She stared at him in disbelief. Could he really feel how off kilter Michael's arrival has made her.

"Yes. Yes I did." Anthony confirmed without an ounce of regret in his tone. She actually thought she heard pride.

Michael tilted his head slightly, pausing to absorb Anthony's innuendo.

"Anthony, I understand you feel the need to mark territory. I also want you to understand that I will treat you and Terry, as I will everyone else here, with respect. And I demand the same." He turned his attention to Terry. "You will be respected both professionally and personally." His voice dropped just a bit when he spoke his last word.

"So, gentlemen, I guess that settles it all." Terry spoke up before any more challenges could be issued. And before her mind could make more of Michael's statement than she wanted it to. Moving around her desk to practically stand between them, she tried to bring this meeting to a quiet end. "Anthony and I are looking forward to seeing the fruits of your labor here." She glanced over her shoulder at Anthony and rushed on at the look on his face. "Just ask your near genius team here to help at anytime and we'll do what we can. Time, desire and resources permitting of course." Both she and Michael broke into a light laugh while Anthony just smirked.

This small insertion of humor seemed to have dissipated a major portion of the tension that had built up in the room. But the cloud was still pretty thick.

Michael moved closer to Terry and extended his hand. Terry glanced at his hand and considered backing away but would not dare wimp out. She quickly and firmly clasped his hand and just as quickly released it. Moving aside, she motioned for him to move forward to Anthony.

"I look forward to working with the two of you. I know we will do great things together." Michael offered.

"Great things huh?" Anthony looked over to Terry as he shook the outstretched peace offering. "How about almost genius?"

"I am definitely up for that." Michael smiled at his sarcastic jest. "I'll leave you to your day now. I am sure everyone is waiting with bated breath to talk with me."

"You'll be fine. They'll warm up to you when they know you are sincere about the company going forward as a whole with your supportive leadership and not by dictatorship." Terry reassured him.

"That is definitely how I operate. Have a great day." And with that, Michael turned and left the room.

Anthony walked over to the window and stood quietly thinking. She knew something was coming but did not expect what happened next. So taking the quiet moment to regroup, Terry moved behind her desk and opened the file she was working on before Michael came in. She kept Anthony in her peripheral vision, expecting him to approach her and the subject of their guest at any moment. But Anthony, quietly walking towards the door, grabbed her full attention. She didn't raise her head from the file but she was locked into Anthony's silent exit from her office. Only, he did not leave. He softly closed the door and then stood there with his back resting against it until Terry closed the file, put down her pen and looked up to where he stood.

"What?" she sighed.

"Tell me."

"Tell you what?" Terry asked as she sat back in her seat.

Anthony's thoughtful composure shifted and became colored with irritation at Terry's bland response.

"Are you seriously going to act like that did not just happen?" He didn't raise his voice, but his tone spoke volumes. When she didn't immediately respond he approached her desk making it clear what he wanted to hear. "Tell me what that,,,, that was between the two of you. And don't you dare say nothing. We've worked together for three years and known each other for four. And there is no way that I'm going to walk around here like I'm blind to the fact that you and Michael Jacobs have a past. And a major one from the looks of it all."

Terry labored to keep her breathing steady and her eyes from running from her friend's piercing stare.

"I don't want to talk about it." Terry rose from her seat and turned from him.

"The hell you don't!" Anthony smacked the top of her desk with his palm, startling her.

Terry spun around to face him. She had never seen Anthony this passionate about another man being in her life. Past or present. She stared into his eyes, trying to decide if his reaction was legitimate concern for his friend or jealousy. Which she completely would not believe.

"You wait one minute." She said holding up her hands to stop this conversation from escalating any higher. She took a deep breath. "I don't know what is happening with you right now, but I do believe you need to get yourself together.   I know we're more than simple colleagues. We are friends. Family even. But understand me, I run my own life.   And if I do not want to talk about something uncomfortable, I won't. Are we clear?"

"Uncomfortable?   I'd say it's much deeper than that." Not backing down, Anthony challenged her rebuke.

"Man, what is it with you?   I do not need this right now."   Her composure was slipping. She picked up her file and slapped it down on her keyboard.

Anthony sat down in the seat vacated by Michael just minutes earlier.

"Um hmm." He now had his confirmation. "Whatever the history is between the two of you, I need to know at least the basics of the situation."

"Anthony, my past has nothing to do with you."

"I disagree. He's our boss and you have a past with this man. And I'm not walking into this blind and without any heads up. You owe me that much."

"Anthony,"

"No Terry. I've been with you for four years straight. Through any and everything," he paused. "Business and personal."

"Anthony, listen to me."

"I said no. Not this time. You're not in this alone. With this business or your life."   He stood and walked over to where she still stood behind her desk and leaned on it facing her. "I told you years ago, you've been adopted. Irreversibly, completely, and wholeheartedly. We are family. Now spill it."

Anthony was very serious when it came to his family. His mother and father, Victouria and Hickman Broder, divorced when he was twelve. His only sister Mikki was sixteen at the time and had an extremely hard time with her father leaving their home. She was a daddy's girl and it was heartbreaking to her. But Anthony became angry when he saw how his father hurt "Their Girls".

CHAPTER TEN
ANTHONY

Because he traveled with work so much, Hickman drilled into Anthony to "be there for the girls while I'm away. Don't let anything happen to them. They are our girls and our responsibility. You are the man of house when I'm gone, so you keep your guard up". He heard repeatedly that he was to be a steadfast protector of his mother and sister. No matter who the offender is, you stand your ground and fight for them. So when Hick left, Anthony was on post and became almost obsessive in his new role as man of the house. But love has a funny way of breaking your focus and your resolve.

Anthony lost his only sister when he was twenty-two in an automobile accident. She wasn't even supposed to be in town to be in harm's way. But Anthony did something stupid, causing his family to panic. He felt responsible for everything.

Mikki Broder was scheduled to leave town on business the morning of April 18. But she delayed her trip for two days because of Anthony's car accident the night before.

A senior at USC Berkeley and home on spring break for the week, he had hung out with his girlfriend Jessica almost everyday. But he promised his favorite uncle that he'd go fishing today so they could catch up. He got back to his mom's house shortly after six to shower and head over to Jessica's. But since his break was almost up, his mom, Victouria, cooked the one dish she could always bribe him with. Her famous mac-n-cheese. He definitely was not going to skip out on dinner with that on the menu. Her plan worked perfectly and she was able to spend some alone time with her baby boy. She missed him terribly while he was away at school.

He showed up at his girlfriend's house around 8:20. Unannounced. That's how he saw her exit the car that belonged to Josh Meadows, her supposedly ex-boyfriend, after a long goodnight kiss. By the time she stepped onto her front porch, Anthony was standing in the middle of the street with his heart breaking.

"Jessica!" He yelled out her name from the pit of his stomach. She spun around and her hand flew to her mouth. "What the hell are you doing Jessica!" Her ex-boyfriend jumped out of his car as soon as Anthony started moving towards her.

"Anthony, what are you doing here?" Jessica asked looking back and forth between him and Josh.

"I thought I was coming to see MY girlfriend!" Anthony yelled. Anthony stopped in his tracks when he saw Josh reach Jessica's side and reach for her hand. She didn't pull away. This incredibly heavy feeling seemed to engulf his entire chest and he felt like he couldn't breathe. When Josh pulled Jessica behind him and he saw her take Josh's protective shielding, he became overwhelmed by his stomach's urge to rebel and broke into a sweat. With tears beginning to pool in his eyes, he turned away and quickly walked back to his car. He wouldn't dare let her see him shed one single tear. He grabbed the handle to open the door but ran to the back of the car to give up the dinner his mother had just blessed him with. This assault on his body was so violent he nearly fell to his knees.

When he was able to right himself, he pulled his polo shirt over his head and wiped his face. He looked back one last time to find Jessica's porch empty. But the sight of Jessica and Josh's silhouettes coming through the thin living room curtains was evidence enough that his relationship was over.

He jumped into his car and was pulling away from the curb before he even closed his door.

He was driving on autopilot on course for home. A mile away from his house, he realized where he was headed and that he couldn't face his mother right now. At the last minute, he decided to get on the freeway to head towards the beach. He had to jump from the middle lane to make the turn and didn't see the SUV in his blind spot on his right.

"Jesus!"

His cry for help and the weightless feeling overtaking him were the last things he remembered before waking up to voices barking out orders all around him. His body felt so heavy and his head was pounding.

"Mom? Oh God. What's happening?" He managed to get out as he opened his eyes. "Mr. Broder. Anthony?" He turned his eyes to the nurse standing near his head. He started to panic when he couldn't turn his head. But he calmed down at the news that his head was just in a brace to keep it stabilized until they were certain he was okay. More of what happened came back to his memory the more she talked. Continuing, she explained the extent of his injuries.

"You've been in a pretty bad car accident. So far, you've gotten out amazingly with only a bruised rib, and three broken fingers. Your legs look fine. You just have some minor lacerations on them and your arms. But you have a pretty bad bruise on your face so we're sending you down for a CT scan."

"My mom. Where's my mom?" he asked as soon as she finished talking.

"We've reached your mom and she's on the way here. Unless you're in CT, we'll bring her back to see you as soon as she gets here."

Anthony closed his eyes again to brace against the pain in his side.

Victouria arrived just after they took him to get his CT scan. His sister was in the middle of packing for her conference when she got the call from her mom telling her to get to the hospital as quickly as possible. Her little brother had just been in an accident. Mikki was as scared as any sister would be, praying the whole drive over to the hospital. But she also had a moment where she remembered that Anthony did not always think first before he acted. And if this was one of those times, once she made sure he was okay, she was going to smack him just for making them worry over him again.

The same nurse that explained everything to Anthony lead Victouria and Mikki to his room shortly after he returned from his test. She explained his condition to them but told them they would have to talk to Anthony about what happened before the accident. The police are going to want to talk with him also. "All I can tell you is he was mumbling the name Jessica and one other word. Why." She hunched her shoulders and opened the door to the room he was in and left them to talk.

The bruise on his face was pretty dark by then and his mother gasped when she entered the room. "Oh, baby are you alright?" She rushed to him to kiss his head.

"Ant! Boy you gotta stop making us worry over you!" His sister said with tears of relief running down her face. He was the most important man in both their lives. And although they didn't hesitate to pull his collar when he needed it, they loved Anthony just as hard and spoiled him even now at this age.

"I'm sorry Mom. Mikki. I didn't mean to get into a jam. It just threw me....," his words drifted off.

His mom spoke first. "What threw you? And what did it have to do with Jessica?"

"Yeah Ant. Tell us what happened." Mikki chimed in sarcastically.

"Mom, I...," He wondered how they knew about his girlfriend. And just how much they knew.

"Anthony, what's done needs to be done." That was her way of telling him to let something go.

He didn't know why, but it took a long time for Jessica to grow on his mother. "I guess now I know why," he thought to himself.

"I rolled up on her with someone else."

Mikki jumped in here. "It was that Josh guy wasn't it?" She went on before he could answer. "I knew she was still seeing him. I just couldn't prove it. But what I did see was enough. You have to learn how to listen to your big sister. I have never lead you wrong Ant."

"Mikki, hold on baby. He's a grown man now." Victouria turned back to Anthony. "Honey, you can't let other people change your life like this." She lifted her hands and motioned for him to take in the hospital room where they were now sitting.

"I know Ma. But it was like I was standing in the middle of a bad dream with a car sitting in the middle of my chest." Men weren't supposed to cry but he could not hold back the tears that were escaping his eyes. He looked up at his sister and confessed. "I've never let anyone this close. Not since dad."

Mikki leaned in and gently hugged his neck, letting her tears fall with his.

CHAPTER ELEVEN

They hadn't openly talked about their father in six years. It was the week Anthony scored the most points of the basketball season by any player in his district, pushing his varsity squad to the finals. His dad promised to make that last game of the season. It was the only one he would finally be able to clear his schedule for. Anthony played his heart out but his dad was nowhere to be seen. He was a no call, no show. That was a Thursday. Two days later, Mikki came running into the house about 5:30, slamming stuff around and yelling about someone getting married and not bothering to tell her. Anthony wondered who he'd have to step to now for hurting his sister's feelings. He wasn't in too much of a hurry since he knew most of the time his sister was normally the heart breaker but got mad if her ex would move on quicker than she thought they should.

He tuned her out to finish the round on the video game he was playing until he heard his name. He dropped his game controller with irritation and made his way to the kitchen where he found his mother holding Mikki is her arms while she cried.

"Why doesn't he love us anymore?" Mikki asked her mother, wiping tears from her face. Then Victouria turned and locked saddened eyes with Anthony.

"Who?" That was all Anthony could get past the knot that was forming in his throat. There was only one person that could make his mom's eyes look sad.

"Baby, come here. I need to talk to you."

He didn't move but said softly, "Just say it."

Mikki took over. "You know that bum people call our father? Well he just happened to get married today. And we weren't even invited!" By the time she was finished, she was yelling again.

Anthony just stood there with his heart breaking and tears filling his eyes. He was standing with his hands balled into fists at his side and breathing so hard and fast he was getting lightheaded. Then he erupted, screaming at the top of his lungs, "I hate him!"

From then on, Victouria and Mikki were his world. Until he met Jessica. It took years for someone to break his protective shell but she became one of "His Girls". He couldn't understand why his mother and sister never fully accepted that. Until now.

Anthony was in the hospital for two days after his accident because of the trauma to his head. Mikki spent a lot of the time on the phone working on the arrangements for the conference she was supposed to leave for before his accident. The evening he came home she said her goodbyes, exchanging hugs and kisses with her mother. For laughs, she snapped a few blackmail pictures of her and Anthony in his remaining bandages.

"Behave yourself," she told him, playfully punching him on his good arm. "Or these photos just may make an appearance on your student union announcement board with a very special caption."

Knowing she'd never embarrass him, he playfully responded, raising his eyebrow suggestively, "We will see. I do have your diary from the ninth grade."

"You wouldn't." Mikki dared. Then she remembered. "No, you couldn't. Because that one was "destroyed" at cheerleading camp," she said slowly with a mischievous grin. "See you next month Ant." She winked, kissed his forehead and turned to leave.

"Whatever! Bye!" Anthony playfully tossed a pillow at the door as it closed behind her laughter.

At three thirty-eight a.m., the house phone rang, waking them with a jolt. Victouria's nerves had not completely settled from Anthony's accident so her heart was already racing. Anthony rose to check on his mother.

"NO!" Victouria's yell stopped Anthony outside her bedroom door as he was coming to see what was so urgent. His heart froze and he couldn't move. Barely breathing, he stood there listening to his mother's side of the conversation. His legs grew weak and his stomach felt sick enough to erupt all over again.

"Where?! Where's my baby?" Victouria cried out.

"Mikki?"   Anthony whispered his sister's name and had to brace
himself on the doorway outside his mother's room.

"What do you mean you're sorry?!"   Victouria's voice trailed off to
almost a whisper.

Anthony sunk to the floor with his arms wrapped around his body. He
sat for what seemed like an hour but in reality was only a minute,
breathing deeply to fight the nausea and dizziness that was attacking
him.

"Anthony!"   Victouria's voice broke him out of his trance and he
rushed into her room to see her standing beside her bed visibly
shaking. When he reached her, she collapsed in his arms sobbing out
the tale told to her by the caller.

Mikki was about thirty minutes away from the hotel she was going to
stay in when a drunk driver turned into her path, colliding with her car
and pushing her into a tree on the other side of the road.

Anthony stood there holding his mother tight, afraid to let her let go
from his embrace. She was all that he had left is all his heart could
feel at that moment.

When he did release his mother, she sunk onto her bed. He dropped
to her feet and she held his head in her lap while his tears soaked her
gown.

He missed two weeks of classes. Determined to make his mother
accept his decision not to return to school, he sat alone in his room for
two days after Mikki's funeral. When he finally came out to eat, he
saw the fresh tears in his mother's eyes. He couldn't take being the
cause of any grief to her after the divorce. So when he saw the tears
fall from her face, he had to try and fix whatever was wrong. And he
took the next few days to get anything and everything done that his
mother needed. He would spend his time at home making sure that
everything was in order for her.

He was wounded by infidelity and loss. He kept his mother close to
his heart but no other woman would ever hurt him again. Oh, he

dated. But that's all it was. He made no commitments and gave no apologies. He treated his lady friends well. But when they did not want to hang out or stay in his game anymore, he let them quickly move on. He made sure he always had two or three available options at all times.

When he met Terry, they quickly became friends. He initially approached her to see if she would fit into his no commitment, fringe benefits world. But he was quickly reminded of his sister Mikki. They talked and vibed like old friends. He was careful at first. Or so he thought. After a year of pretending she was just like one of the guys to him, Terry was offered a job out of state. He felt like he was about to lose a part of his world and had to admit to himself and to Terry how important and how much like family she was to him. It was odd and strange to him to love her so deeply and not have any romantic intent.

Knowing how he was with women, and being caught off guard by Anthony's feelings, Terry made her schedule busier than usual. She wanted to make sure that she would not get caught up in his world. But when Anthony realized what she was doing, he flew his mother in and had them meet at his house for dinner. Thirty minutes after meeting, Victouria walked over to Terry and took both of her hands. Looking over at Anthony, and with tears forming in her eyes, she whispered, "I see why she means so much to you." She looked back at Terry and said, "It is completely my privilege to have met you."

That evening they sat and ate and talked about Mikki and Anthony to Victouria's heart's content. From then on, Terry became an honorary Broder and one of Anthony's "Girls".

CHAPTER TWELVE
MONDAY: BACK TO THE PRESENT

"Anthony." Terry sat in the seat beside him. "Look, I don't want to drag my baggage into this room right now."

Anthony opened his mouth to talk but she stopped him.

"Truth is, with all that has been going on for the past week, I just can't talk about this right now. It's taking all that I have to stay focused and, really, just sane." She paused to think for a moment. "Just suffice it to say that we did have a past. And, it ended really bad. It took a long time and a lot of work to get over it. And I do not want to relive it. I don't know why he is here at this company, at this time, this week,,," she sat shaking her head and trying to process her thoughts. "All I do know is that I survived everything that has been thrown my way. And I am not going to let anything or anyone stop what we are working to accomplish."

"Look Terry, I'm with you. OK? And I've got your back." He sat forward in his chair and looked her in the eye. "Are you sure you can handle this? Do you need me to do anything? And, how much can we trust what this man says? You let me know what I need to do and I will handle it." Anthony declared.

"I know you will. But don't tear down any walls just yet. Okay?" Terry said jokingly. "I'm good. Seriously, I am."

"Yeah, okay." He replied with a smile, softening the serious look on his face. "One day, when you are ready, I'd love to hear what a fool he was."

"You have all the info you need already. He let me get away didn't he?"

"Yeah. A fool and stupid. And he wants to run this department? Hmp." Anthony shook his head and rose to leave. "Alright. Let me know when you get the prints from Creative. I have a lunch date to get to." He raised his eyebrows repeatedly and headed out of her office.

"You are so bad."

"Yeah, and you love me anyway. See you after lunch." He disappeared down the hall.

The rest of the day passed without any more upheavals. After returning from lunch, Anthony checked on Tadashi but did not have any updates on the status of the contract.

Although disappointed, Terry pushed forward and they finished their presentation just after seven.

"Alright Anthony, that's it. We are ready to present. Leave a message for Kayla to call Boston and set a meeting immediately. I want to get this project up and rolling as quickly as possible."

"Will do. Let's get that check in the bank ahead of schedule. Clayton just loves it when we cram more revenue on the books."

"Yes. Yes he does. So, line item two, Schafer's, is on the table for tomorrow. Two big checks in one week sounds "Genius" to me!" They both burst into laughter and slapped hands.

"Let's get out of here, I'm starving." Terry turned to invite Anthony to join her while unsuccessfully stifling a sarcastic giggle. "And uh, unless you have a dinner date too, you are more than welcome to join little ole me for a meal. I'm feeling fajitas tonight. Or is that what you had for lunch?"

"Really Terry?"

"Oh sin- cerely dear Anthony." She couldn't hold back her laughter any longer. Grabbing her purse, she sashayed by him dramatically.

"You are so lucky mom has you under her protection." Anthony declared as he closed the door to her office behind her.

"And just what is that supposed to mean?" Terry asked with mock innocence.

"That means she just saved you from being put across my knee young lady."

"Wow. Young lady. No one has called me that in a long time."

"Yeah, and I know why. And only I, your brother who loves you dearly, can tell you." Anthony replied with a sober face.

Terry stopped in the middle of the hallway and turned to Anthony with her hands on her hips.

"Well, excuse me. So why is that?"

Anthony's face turned instantly from innocent to "Uh oh, maybe I should not have asked" mischievous.

"Because your granny panties are making you feel old. But if you dressed like I saw in the picture from the wedding on Saturday more often, you just might get you some."

Terry's mouth flew open and she slapped his arm in protest. "Really?! Man I don't believe you! I am not like you. Must your mind always be so close to the gutter?" She spun away from the deep laughter that erupted from him and stomped off to the elevator. It opened quickly and she was going to let it close on him but Anthony shoved his briefcase in the door.

She stood in the back of the elevator frowning at Anthony through their reflections. Anthony, however, was doing a very poor job at stifling his laughter. She was so glad the office was empty.

Or so she thought. What Terry could not see was that Michael had heard them coming from the opposite side of the hall and had stopped to wait for them to leave. He didn't want to cause her any more stress than he already had that day. Besides, he was a little curious about her and Anthony's relationship and he had decided earlier in the day to be very observant when it came to those two.

"Brother, huh? Well, I guess I have my answer," he thought with a slight smile on his face. Maybe there was a chance for them to reconnect. He knew it would be a long shot but any relationship would be better than not being able to talk with her at all. He missed her more and more each year. He hated how he left her so long ago. It was the worst mistake he'd ever made. He wanted that love back. And any part of it would do. For now.

Terry drifted off to sleep last night around ten thirty. After leaving the office, she and Anthony decided to stop a block away at a restaurant that served a mixture of Mexican and American items on their menu. She had eaten there before but this was her first time going there for dinner. Feeling more like her old self, she decided to try something different. Not too different, but just enough to tease her taste buds. She believed you should always try to enjoy your dining experiences to the fullest. After all, you are paying for it. Her food was good, although she did little more than pick at it once she took a few hefty bites. It was definitely going home with her. Anthony even talked her into trying the Sangria, of which she drank only a few swallows. It did not go to waste though. Anthony was not hearing that. He polished it off before they left. The rest of her evening passed quietly.

After her shower, she sat at her vanity to read her Bible before she turned in. When she was finished, she stretched beneath her covers and felt her body really relax.

"Well God, today was a good day. It had its challenges. But after the last few days, it looks like things are settling down. Thank you for tomorrow. Good night." Then it was lights out.

CHAPTER THIRTEEN
TUESDAY

"What is that? Why is the ringing so loud?"

"Owww! Why are you hitting me! Stop! STOP!"

The ringing was so loud it was making her head pound. Terry looked down. She stood soaked in a pool of water, bent over in pain from the assault on her stomach.

"Nooooo!" Terry sat straight up in her bed. Her covers were halfway on the floor and she was covered in sweat and breathing like she had just run around the block. She quickly looked around the room. It wasn't real. It was just a weird dream. But as soon as she realized her phone wasn't actually ringing, she discovered that the ringing was coming directly from between her ears. Her head was pounding. "Oh Jesus," she whispered, then looked over at the clock on her nightstand. It was 3:03 am. Suddenly she doubled over on the bed as a pain erupted in her abdomen that just consumed her. It was so intense, it took her breath away. She tried to get up to go to the bathroom but immediately fell to the floor. She hated bad dreams but she wished that was all that this was at that moment.

This was not right. She had never experienced anything like this before. Terry felt around for her phone and dialled 911. It was hard for her to listen to what the dispatcher was saying through the cloud of the pain in her stomach. She just started talking between her gasps for air, saying her name and address, and that there was really bad pain in her stomach. "It hurts. Please, it hurts." She heard the words "on the way" and a cry of relief escaped her mouth. She dropped the phone and in what seemed like forever, crawled to her bedroom door and slid herself down the stairs. She managed to make it over to unlock the front door just moments before the Ambulance pulled up and the EMT ran up the townhouse steps.

The EMT's worked quickly to assess her condition, pulling out of her what they could about her pain. They attached her to the monitors and loaded her into the truck for the sprint to the hospital.

Her mind was reeling. Alternating between fighting to stay alert through the pain, and trying to take in all that was being said and done. The coolness of the oxygen coming through her face mask felt so good against her hot face. "God please. Just make it stop," she prayed. Fear was screaming, "This is it! You thought it was over. Well now it is." She could hear the heart monitor beeping faster. And she felt panic start to take over as the next wave of pain hit.

Terry closed her eyes and tried to breathe through it. She began to whisper another prayer and checking her heart. She believed she was straight with God. But in a situation like this, she thought, when you have the chance it doesn't hurt to make sure. She didn't live far from the hospital but it's amazing how fast the mind and how slow time can move at the same time in a crisis. Then prayer's calming effect began to still her mind. Under normal circumstances, she knew how to quickly find and shift to that special place in God where she found peace. Even though she was in excruciating pain, she recognized the opportunity and seized that moment to focus on the one name that is above all names. She repeated over and over in her head, "Jesus! Jesus! I have to be ready. No matter... no matter what is happening in my body." Terry gasped through her pain, "Ah, oh God. Mmmmm. Please let me have peace in this."

Really? You're giving up? Again?

The words were so quiet, yet crystal clear at the same time.

Terry immediately opened her eyes. Tears were now running down the sides of her face. She focused on one spot on the ceiling of the truck and whispered into her oxygen mask, "No!"

Terry made her mind shift. With every pain she whispered through the fog a thank you for healing, recovery, protection, and anything else she could grasp past the pain. It was not easy to focus. And those last few minutes of the ride felt like they were dragging. More tears, this time of relief, ran down her face when they arrived at the hospital and the doors opened for them to whisk her into the building.

The nurses quickly got her situated and performed all of their preliminary vital checks so the doctor could complete his examination as soon as she was slipped into her room. They did an ultrasound, drew blood and sent it for testing.

They also did an ICE search, In Case of Emergency, on her cellphone to find her emergency contact.

An hour passed before Angela entered the room where Terry was resting. By then, whatever they put in her IV was making her pain subside.

She knew it was Angela's hand on her forehead before she even opened her eyes. The scent of Angela's favorite lotion registered through her exhaustion and woke her.

When she opened her eyes, she saw Angela's eyes closed and her lips moving. In prayer, she was sure. She looked peaceful. Her presence was always calming, even when she herself was upset. Terry didn't know how that could be, but somehow that is just how it was with Angela.

"Angela," Terry whispered. Angela's eyes flew open and the tears she was holding back escaped. She quickly rose from her seat next to the bed and threw her arms as far around Terry as she could.

For the second time in their friendship, Angela was true to her name. Being there as the rock for her to cling to when she opened her eyes. Waiting patiently by Terry's side like an angel on watch.

"Hey Baby-cakes. How are you feeling?" Angela slid her cool hand across Terry's forehead.

"I'm much better. You haven't called me that in years." Although she'd never admit it, Terry loved it when Angela "mothered" her.

"And you haven't scared me like that in years either. You know my nerves are already on high alert where you are concerned. And then I get a call from the hospital about you. They don't tell you anything over the phone. Just get here as soon as you can!" Angela mocked the nurse that made the call to her.

"Yeah, I'm sorry. This time was definitely not on purpose. Trust me."

"I know hon. But it is still nerve racking. You just have way too much going on with you this week. I don't know how much more I can take. Have they told you anything?"

"All I know is that the pain is gone and they are waiting for test results. They took plenty of blood too. I started to ask the nurse if she was trying to be a vampire or something weird." They both laughed at her bad joke.

"I see the clown in you is just fine."

"Well, I'll be much better once I find out what happened, and how to keep it from ever happening again. I don't ever, ever ever, ever ever ever, want to feel anything like that, ever again in my life." Terry made her feelings very clear.

"Wow. Now that's bad."

"Didn't you hear me say "Ever"?" Terry reiterated.

"Okay. What did it feel like? Tell me what happened." Angela slipped her hand around Terry's fingers.

"Ange, all I know is that I was sleeping good. And then I was dreaming something awful. There was a ringing in my head. And I thought I was getting hit in my stomach. I don't remember much more of the details. But I do know it felt real. And it turned out that it was."

"So real it woke you?"

"So real I can't wait for the doctor to tell me what caused it so I never have it happen again. I don't think I can say that enough to express to you the depth of my never gonna do that again commitment."

Angela laughed again at the expression on Terry's face.

"I hear you Sister. Let me see if I can get any information from the nurses out there." Angela rose to leave the room.

"And look here, if anybody gives you a hard time, you send them directly to me. Cause I needs to know something asap." Terry commanded.

"Yes Ma'am." Angela saluted.

"Now who's the smarty pants?" Both ladies broke into laughter and Angela left her E.R. room.

Terry had been resting her eyes for several minutes and was actually about to drift into a light sleep when she heard her door open. Assuming Angela had returned, she resisted the urge to sink deeper into her rest in favor of getting her anticipated answers. She opened her eyes. But she was surprised by who stood in front of her.

"Terry? Oh dear, it is you. What happened?" The woman questioned.

"Patrice? What are you doing here? Did something happen with Jarod?"

"Oh no. He's fine. Every month I volunteer a few days here as a nurse."

"Wow. That's pretty impressive. But not too surprising."

"Really?" Patrice questioned.

"Yes. I could tell that your compassion was genuine when I met you last week." A smile formed on Terry's mouth.

"Well, thank you. I've been blessed to have Jarod make sure I never really have to work anymore. But I still enjoy being here and helping people. This way I can help in a way that I know counts."

"More than a pen stroke in your checkbook. That's good to know."

Patrice stepped closer to the bedside. "Don't get me wrong. We have contributed quite a bit of money to the hospital. I worked here with many of these nurses just a few years ago. And I understand the struggle several of them have. So it also gives me the opportunity to help them out by donating a day's work."

"Wow. You don't see that often."

"You don't see that ever." Patrice laughed. "Maybe I'll start a trend."

"Ha! Don't hold your breath." Terry replied with sarcasm.

"I know. But one could hope." Patrice said. However, the look on her face showed exactly how she really felt about that happening.

They both laughed and Patrice took the seat near Terry's bed.

"So tell me what happened. But, only if you don't mind sharing. I know we've only just met."

"Don't worry. It's not related to what happened with the car. At least I don't believe it is. And no one has told me different." Terry tried to reassure Patrice.

"Please don't misunderstand me dear. I'm only concerned with your well being. All that happened on Friday will work itself out. Here, I may be able to help. Now tell me. What brought you here?"

"I woke up with really bad pains in my stomach area. It was like nothing I've ever experienced before. And I was really scared. So I called 911."

"Have they given you a diagnosis?"

"No. Not yet. My friend Angela just went to look for someone. I do know they did an ultrasound and took blood but I don't have any results yet."

"Well, since I'm here, let me see what I can do to move things along." Patrice offered with a wink.

"Patrice you don't have to do that."

"Nonsense. You rest and I'll be back as soon as I can."

Before Patrice could leave, Angela walked into the room.

"Terry, I wasn't able..." Angela stopped when she saw the nurses uniform. "Oh great, you're already here. Did you already give her the test results?"

Terry interrupted, "Angela, this is Patrice. Patrice Lewis."

"Oh. Hello." Angela looked from one woman to the other. "That's odd."

A confused look settled on Patrice's face. "Odd? What do you mean?
"

"Um. I don't mean to offend you or jeopardize Terry's care, but should
the wife of the guy who almost seriously hurt her be her nurse?"

"Angela!" Shocked, Terry sat up in her bed.

"I'm sorry Terry. You know how I am when it comes to you." Angela
turned her attention back to Patrice. "Look, like I said, I'm not trying to
be mean or rude. Terry can usually handle herself. But right now
she's on her back and needs back up. And I'm it. So I have to ask."
Angela defended her stance.

"Angela, come on. Are you really embarrassing me like that?"

 "Terry, it's ok." Patrice moved closer to the ladies. "I understand
where Angela is coming from. Sometimes It's hard to not go
overboard when the well being of the people you love is at risk."

"Ok, but still. Angela, I'd expect something like that from Leighann,
but this isn't like you."

"Ladies," Patrice interrupted again. "I'm going to check on your test
results and give you some privacy." Patrice patted Terry's hand with
an understanding smile. "Don't be too hard on her," she instructed
softly, then she left the room.

"Angela..."

"I'm sorry Terry. Really." Angela took a deep breath to calm herself.
"I didn't mean to embarrass you. But you know how things can go
wrong when you don't ask the right questions. I've lost too much in
my life already. You know how I lost...Carl. I didn't even get the
chance to fight for him. Just one day, he was gone." She still found it
hard to talk about her deceased husband. She took another deep

breath and continued on. This time her voice softer. "And you, you were a close call once. And it scared the life out of me."

"Angela, I understand being worried and all, but you were way over the top here. For you, that was Leighann high. Heck, I can even see Kristine going a little ham in here. But you? You're my rock. And you don't shake that easily."

"I said I'm sorry, alright. I've had some stuff going on myself and I'm just..." Angela had this lost look momentarily cross her face.

"Just what? What happened with you?" Terry sat up straighter.

"I'm ok. We need to focus on you right now." Angela tried to take Terry's focus off of her. She just wasn't ready to talk about her current issue. There would be time for that later.

"Angela, I'm surrounded by health professionals. And I'm going to be fine. But if you want me to stay calm, you need to start talking."

"It's not a big deal. Really. I'm just making it bigger than it is because I was caught off guard. And my nerves were already on end with all this stuff with you going on." Terry crossed her arms and waited for her to continue. Looking to the floor, Angela took a deep breath and with carefully planned words, pushed on. "I had this new client show up today and it was very stressful. That's all. But I...I don't want to focus on that right now. I can't focus on that right now."

"Hey." Terry squeezed her hand to get her attention. "We can talk about it if you need to. Angela?" Angela sat silent for several seconds. Her eyes began to tear up.

"Angela, honey? What is going on?" Terry shifted until she was eye to eye with her. "Something is not right. You better tell me right now or I'm calling in the cavalry. And you know she is always packing."

A slight smile rested on Angela's face at the thought of Leighann bursting through the door with guns blazing.

"I know right!" Terry had the same picture pop in her head. "I can see it now. The nurses all hunched under the desk. And a cloud of smoke floating down the hallway floor." Angela was laughing so hard now that she couldn't keep the tears from rolling down her cheeks.

"Oh, and don't forget the matrix black trench coat and four inch black red bottoms. 'Cause you got to look Boss when kicking behind.' " Angela mocked her friend, barely keeping a straight face. "I have never seen anything like her."

"And you never will. And you know she definitely did not use the word, behind."

"Girl, you know it. That child is a walking cuss box! If you ain't heard it, just make her mad. She'll pull out her personal cuss thesaurus. You are gonna learn a few things, and a few cuss combinations you never thought existed," Angela agreed.

"You'll feel like you need to go on a 24 hour consecration. And you weren't even the one doing the talking," Terry countered.

They were laughing so hard, one of the nurses poked her head in to see what the commotion was.

"Well ladies, it looks like our patient is feeling much better." The nurse walked over to the room's computer and went through the routine of updating Terry's vital information.

Angela sat quietly so the nurse could get an accurate blood pressure reading. Just as she was pulling the cuff off, Patrice walked into the room.

"Hi Carol. Terry, the doctor should be on his way in to see you with your test results."

"Great! Thank you. Thank you so much."

"It was no problem. He'll be here shortly. So I'll step out so you can have your privacy." Patrice patted Terry's hand and turned to Angela. "Have a good day. She'll be fine."

"Thank you Patrice. And I'm sorry for being so rude," Angela apologized.

"Honey, if that's all you've got, I think I got off easy." Patrice gave Angela a wink, letting her off the hook. "Take care. Terry, if you are still here when I finish my shift, I'll check in on you before I leave."

"Ok. See you later."

Angela sat down again next to Terry's bed.

"She is pretty nice," Angela admitted.

"I told you so," Terry responded. Innocently forgetting what challenge came along with those four words.

"Whatever Terry." Angela sat back in her seat and crossed her leg while letting a mischievous smirk spread across her face.

"Oh no. We are not playing the told you so game. I sincerely apologize." Terry spoke soberly.

"And?"

"Come on Angela. I thought you loved me like I was your very own. And I already said I was sorry." Terry pleaded softly.

Angela lowered her voice, put on her Leighann the Queen pose and did her best impression of their friend. "Well, since I've already unleashed a small portion of the bad girl in me, and I probably won't ever get another chance to let my inner Leighann flow, I feel it is my duty to give you a loving hard time. Angela style."

"Because of one I Told You So? Come on!" Terry was laughing so hard she was in tears. "No one, but no one, can dish out a told you so beat down like Leigh. She is so crafty on so many levels. How could you ever do her justice?"

Lifting her head higher, Angela was fighting hard to keep a straight face.

"I don't know.   But since we are waiting until later today to tell her anything about what is going on, thereby sparing the staff of this wonderful establishment her wrath, it is my duty to at least give you what I would consider the highlights of her take no prisoners, take over this John Brown wing and shut it down if I don't get no answers tirade. I repeat, Angela style of course." She couldn't hold it in any longer and burst out in laughter so hard a few drops of moisture flew out of her mouth.

They both stopped cold, stared at each other and then started laughing all over again.

She was feeling so much better physically and emotionally that Terry lost all thought of pain for the moment. She was so into her funny exchange with Angela that she almost didn't hear the knock on her door.

Wiping the tears from her eyes she answered, "Come in!"

Both ladies instantly fell silent when the doctor entered.

Sweet father! Morris Chestnut chocolate, with Michael Ealy eyes. Daang! You do not see that combination often. Gorgeous!

"Close your mouth child," her mind commanded. "He said something. What did he say? Doctor something. OMG! Look at that smile!" If her thoughts managed to escape her lips right now, she would just pull the covers up over her head and hope to disappear. She stuck her hand out to shake his. "So soft. And warm. Dang! What did they put in this IV?"

Terry heard Angela clear her throat and snapped out of her thoughts.

"I'm so sorry. We were, uh, joking around and I wasn't focused. What did you say your name was again?"

Oh my goodness! Did his smile just get bigger? "I'm Dr. Ryan. And I'm so glad to see that you are feeling better."

"Me too. Whatever you put in that IV bag is working wonders." Terry made light of her former distress. She took that moment to run her fingers through her tresses, a subtle vanity check to make sure her hair was not too dishevelled. She may be in the hospital but that's no reason to look raggedly. Especially at the present moment. Focus, child, focus.

"In this case, we didn't have to give you much. For the most part, your body needed the fluids. You had a few other things going on all at once. But nothing too major." Dr. Ryan tried to assure her.

"Really? Well, I'd truly hate to see what major looks like. I don't think I could take it!" Terry laid back on the bed. She was starting to feel a little tense.

Dr. Ryan took the cue from the change in Terry's mood and pulled the stool over and took a seat. Lowering his height perspective often helped to relax his patients and make the consultation less stressful.

"Ms. Ellis.." Dr. Ryan started. Wait, did he just drop some more bass in his voice. Terry's mind started wandering again.

"Please, call me Terry." The slight smirk on Angela's face said that she heard it too. Oh stop, you're hearing things.

"Alright Terry. What we found can be fixed with rest and diet. Looking through your notes and recent history, I can see that you've had a very stressful week. You have a note here.." He paused to take another look at her chart. "Your initial trigger could have been your anxiety over your recent dental visit." He looked up from her chart.

"Yeah, well, my dentist is nice and he's very gentle. He does great work and I hate going." The fake smile on her face said it all.

"What a special compliment." Dr. Ryan chuckled. "But I do understand where you're coming from. Many patients experience the white coat syndrome response. The doctor walks into their room and immediately their blood pressure shoots to the roof."

"Well, the very thought of going does it for me." Terry confirmed.

"I can attest to that!" Angela spoke up with a little too much enthusiasm.

"Thank you. Thank you very much Mother Angela!" Terry responded sarcastically.

Dr. Ryan laughed with them. "I take it that you, Mother Angela, are the rock in Terry's support circle."

"Yes, Dr. Ryan. I am the leader of her support group," Angela replied smugly.

"Wonderful. Then you are just the person that we need to have in the room." Turning back to his patient, he continued, "Terry, what you will need to do for the next few days is simply lessen your stress, take in plenty of fluids and do not skip meals."

"That's all?" she asked in disbelief.

"Yes ma'am. Let me explain. What you had going on is a combination of stress and dehydration. And although your consumption was minimal, the alcohol didn't help matters. When we are stressed our bodies produce a hormone called cortisol which increases heart rate and blood pressure. And there is also an effect on the metabolic processes such as digestion. That, mixed with the fact that stress causes us to either eat more or not at all, can have a notable impact on the state of our stomachs. You have experienced several stressful events in a very short period of time. And you haven't been taking in enough to regulate your blood sugar or replace your fluids. So we've given you a few supplements and fluids. And I see that has already helped."

"I do feel better." Terry agreed.

"I could tell. You have a nice laugh." Their eye contact lingered for a moment before Dr. Ryan cleared his throat and looked back down to her chart.

Don't read too much into it. Don't do it girl. "Thank you. I, uh," Terry didn't know what to say next. Angela spoke up to help her save face.

"So Doc, how long before she can go home?"

"She's responding well to treatment, so it won't be too long. We'll check her vitals again shortly. If all her readings are as I expect them to be, I'll prepare her discharge instructions."

"Great. Now do you recommend her to stay at home or will she be able to go to work today? I'll need you to make that clear for her especially if you want her to take the day off." Angela sat back in her chair with the sweetest, don't mess with me, smile.

"Thank you Angela." Terry's gratitude was dripping in sarcasm. She was not going quietly home without a fight. "Dr. Ryan, since I'm feeling better, I should be ok going into the office. Right?"

"Instruction No. 1 was to lessen stress," Dr. Ryan reminded her. "What type of work do you do?"

"Public Relations and Media Management. But my partner can easily take on anything stressful for the next day or so." Terry hoped her cheerful explanation would keep the doctor on her side.

Dr. Ryan looked knowingly to Angela. "Ok. I see our patient may need a little more supervision than usual."

"I'm already on it. I will be speaking directly with her partner to make sure that he understands her instructions." Angela turned to Terry, "Big Brother will be watching you."

"Oh, good grief. Fine! I will take it easy. Now can I please go home?" Terry pleaded.

"I will send the nurse in to prepare your information for discharge." Dr. Ryan chuckled. "Mother Angela has got my back." He winked at Angela before he left the room.

"Traitor." Terry labeled her friend with the roll of her eyes.

"Thank you. Thank you very much. Now, we'll get you home and ready for work. Because I know that's exactly where you are going to run to. And while you are getting dressed, I'll make the call to Anthony."

"I can let him know what happened."

"Sure you can. But will you?" Angela challenged.

"Whatever Angela. You are starting to stress me so I'm going to rest my mind." Terry laid her head on her pillow and closed her eyes. "Thank you Jesus," she whispered and Angela reached over and covered her hand. She was going to be just fine and could truly relax.

It took about another thirty minutes to get everything ready for her release. It was near time to shift change and Patrice was true to her word. She stopped in to check on Terry. This time she was welcomed by Angela. She was about to leave when Dr. Ryan knocked and entered with Terry's discharge papers.

"Ok Terry. Here are your discharge instructions. Oh, hi Patrice." Dr. Ryan was a little surprised by Patrice's presence.

"Dr. Mac. How are you?"

"I'm great. I didn't know you were in the E.R. tonight. Terry, it looks like you've had the best care this facility can provide at your side."

"You are too kind. But no, I was just checking on Terry before I head home." She turned back to Terry and Angela. "Ladies, I meant what I said. If you need anything, please do not hesitate to call me."

"I will be fine. But thank you so much for your help tonight. You have a good day."

"I'll take good care of her," Angela chimed in.

"Alright. Good day ladies." Patrice said her goodbye with a soft smile. But her smile widened when she turned to address Dr. Ryan, taking in the papers in his hands. The nurses usually handle that. "Doctor."

"Have a great day Patrice." Dr. Ryan cleared his throat quickly and smiled back before returning his attention to his patient.

"Terry, here are your discharge instructions." He moved close to where she was sitting while being sure to keep a professional distance. He handed her a card and then went through each sheet. He ended with advising her to follow up with her primary physician when he was finished. "And if you have any questions, please do not hesitate to call and leave me a message. If it isn't urgent, of course. I'll be sure to return your call as quickly as possible."

"Thank you. I will." The handsome E.R. doctor was making himself available. Now this day is becoming brighter and the sun hadn't risen high yet.

"Now, since the medical matters are handled," Dr. Ryan continued, switching subjects, "would you mind if I contacted your office sometime. I'd like to pick your brain about a few ideas I have about a personal project I am working on?"

"Um, I guess that would be okay. I don't think that would be a problem." I told you not to read too much into anything, she reminded herself. "Angela, could you hand me a card from my purse?"

Terry took the card and handed it to the doctor. "Thank you very much Terry. I look forward to talking with you under better circumstances. And Angela, I know you'll take great care of her."

"You can bet on that Dr. Ryan."

"Alright Ladies, have a blessed day."

"You too." Both ladies responded together, shaking his outstretched hand before he left the room.

"Alright ! Let's get me out of here. Hand me my clothes please." Terry announced throwing back her covers.

"Yes ma'am. I'm going to the waiting area and call Anthony. You'll be in a couple of hours late this morning."

"Angela, I have just enough time to get ready." Terry protested.

"You heard the doctor. Now hear me. You are going to be delayed a couple of hours this morning. Enough said. I'll see you in the lobby."

Angela proceeded to walk out of the room and closed the door behind her without waiting for a response.

"Oh well. I could use a little nap." No need to fight. Angela always won.

It was just after eight when they left the hospital. Angela announced on the ride home that Anthony would not expect Terry before ten that morning. "I've set two alarms on your phone. One for nine fifteen, and one for ten fifteen. I know you are itching to get into the office but if you need the extra hour, take it."

"Yes ma'am!" Terry saluted.

"Funny Terry. Real funny. Don't play. Okay?" Angela's tone was serious.

"Okay, Okay. I am going to lie down. Promise." Terry laid her head back and closed her eyes. In the few minutes it took to get to her front door, she had already relaxed into a deep sleep. Angela had to shake her several times to wake her. She walked Terry into the house to make sure she got in safely.

"Good day hon. I'll call you later."

"Thanks Ange. Love you girl." Terry closed the door behind her friend and made a beeline up the stairs, leaving a trail of clothes on the floor of her room. A quick shower and straight to the sheets. She was asleep as soon as her head hit her pillow. No more dreams, thankfully.

CHAPTER FOURTEEN

Nine fifteen came too soon and she immediately hit the dismiss button. She was definitely taking the extra hour.

Terry walked into the office at eleven forty-five, just before the quiet of the lunch hour. Anthony appeared in her doorway only seconds after she pushed the power button on her computer.

"Hey Lady. How are you feeling?" He asked.

"Anthony, I'm feeling good. A little tired but I will be just fine. And please don't hover. I know Angela put you on high alert. But I don't need it. I'm staying seated, calm and focused on completing my in-office to do list. You can "go to lunch" now." She made the quote marks in the air.

"I've set a meeting for tomorrow with Maria Henderson to deliver the presentation completed last night. And by the way, I am "having lunch" in my office today and working on the Shafer file. So take this quiet time to get settled in for the day. I will be back after lunch." Anthony smiled sweetly yet sarcastically. Turning on his heel, he walked out of her office, softly closing the door behind him.

"Dang watch dogs." Terry shook her head and smiled softly. She wouldn't have it any other way.

Anthony showed up at exactly one o'clock to check on his charge. Terry was so focused on her computer screen that she didn't hear him enter the room.

"Hey." He spoke, startling her.

"What? Oh, hey. I'm okay."

"I know. What are you working on?"

"I've been doing some research. Did you know that Evan Blake is launching a new product? Because, let me tell you, his last two projects hit a million in sales in less than nine months. Both of them did." Terry's excitement was written all over her face.

"What is it?"

"Don't know yet. But I do know this. He just got back from looking at two large commercial properties in New Mexico."

Anthony already knew the direction her mind was headed. He grabbed the post-it pad from her desk and started writing out an action list. They worked like a well oiled machine for sure. He immediately had four names to call and would have a preliminary report to give her within two hours.

"Alright. Maria may be able to provide a few clues to help us out on this too. I'll be sure to throw out a couple of feelers tomorrow when we talk. Are there any names you want to add to my list?" Anthony asked.

"Just make sure you call Bonita Chambers first."

"You got it. What's up?"

"I just have a feeling she's going to be the best lead on this one. Let me know what you find out." Terry instructed, barely looking away from her screen.

"Ok boss. I'll be back as soon as I know something."

"I'll be right here."

"I know, Angela's orders." He chuckled.

"Whatever man. Go make your phone calls please." Terry brushed him off.

"Yes sir!" Anthony saluted.

Terry spun around in her chair. "You are going to pay for that."

"Sadly, I already am. Babysitting my boss genius." He replied with a mischievous smirk on his face.

"You know you love me." She threw out as she turned her attention back to her computer and waved him on.

"Yeah, but only all day Sunday, Thursday and every other Saturday." He fired back and closed the door on his laughter.

Terry just shook her head and laughed to herself. She couldn't imagine her life without her friend and adopted brother. Now, back to work. "I'm getting this account, whatever it is."

Just moments later there was a soft knock on the door. "Hmm, must have forgotten to give me my final Angela order." She turned her chair to face the door and with a patient expectant smile on her face said, "Come in." But it didn't hold when her door opened.

"Hello."

"Michael? Uh, hello. What can I do for you?" Terry tensed a little.

"I saw that you made it in and just wanted to stop in and check on you." Michael explained.

"Oh, well. Thank you. All is well." She assured him.

"I was told that you were under the weather?" This caught Terry off guard.

"Uh, like I said, I'm fine. There's no reason for you to be concerned."

Michael started to reply but stopped himself. "Alright." But instead of leaving, he walked deeper into the room. Making Terry more uneasy.

"Michael was there something else you needed?" There were no witnesses, so there was no need to wear kid gloves with him.

"I just wanted to see that you were okay." He replied softly.

"I've already told you that I am. Michael, look, I think this is a good time to set some boundaries." She was losing her patience.

"What do you mean?"

Terry released a frustrated sigh and sat back in her seat, crossing her wrists over her crossed knee. She lifted her head high and looked him in the eye. "We're not playing this game. I am not playing this game. I don't know why you chose this company for your next move. But please understand that your personal concern is not needed. We are not friends. Nor will we be. You occupy a superior position at the moment and you will be respected as such. So let me put your mind at ease. I have never fallen short on production dollars in any quarter with this company. And if I am not feeling well, Anthony will always have my back."

"Is that all he has? Your back?" Michael stepped closer to her desk.

His response puzzled her, but only momentarily. So he thinks we're an item. The thought amused her. She stood slowly and placed a slight smile on her face.

"Mr. Jacobs, if I am ever away from the office, Anthony can answer any questions you may have regarding any of our ongoing projects. I thought we made that clear during our meeting on yesterday. I trust him. Implicitly."

"Hey Terry.." Anthony looked up from his notes and stopped abruptly when he saw Michael standing in the office. "Sorry. I didn't mean to interrupt."

"You didn't. I believe Mr. Jacobs was finished." She turned her attention back to Michael. "Thank you for stopping by. And like I said, if you ever need anything and I am not around, just ask Kayla to get Anthony. Or you can seek him out yourself. He'll be more than happy assist you. Won't you Anthony."

"Of course. Anything you need." He responded cautiously.

Michael looked from one to the other. "Very well then. I'm glad you are better. Have a good afternoon." He turned and walked out of the office declaring to himself, "This isn't over. She'll have to talk to me sooner or later."

Anthony waited until Michael was out of sight before he said anything. He closed the office door while Terry took her seat and turned to her computer. Anthony approached her desk and just stood there.

"Anthony, nothing happened. He came in to check on me because someone blabbed and said I was under the weather this morning. We are out of the office on business all the time. So, any idea who felt the need to share that little piece of information?" She looked up into his face.

"It had to be Kayla. She's the only person that I spoke to about why you weren't in."

"Yes, Miss 411. She is the best resource but such a pain when it's my business she chooses to share. I'll have to instruct her on the boundaries I have set where Mr. Jacobs is concerned."

"Mr. Jacobs? I thought we were all on a first name basis. What happened since yesterday?" Anthony questioned.

"Nothing. To be honest, there was no one to put on a show for. So I spoke frankly with him. We have only business to discuss, and for him to be concerned about. He understands and that is the end of the matter."

Anthony stood silently for a moment.

"Well, I still don't like this. It feels like you are holding our careers in the palm of your hand. Playing this little game of yours .."

"There is no game Anthony." She interrupted Anthony's speech. But that only made him more determined to be heard. This time when he spoke there was an edge to his voice. And he repeated his words for maximum effect.

"..Playing this game of yours of, if I ignore it, it will go away, is a sure fire way of setting us up to fail. And you know good and hell well that I do not lose without a fight. So you had better put your boxing gloves on because I am not letting this, thing, you have.."

"Had!" she interrupted again. But he didn't miss a beat.

"Have! ...ruin everything we've worked for." Anthony corrected.

"Nothing is going to be ruined. Michael can not take anything from us." Terry objected.

"Are you even listening to yourself? He already has. This golden boy just swooped in and took your job. Your promotion! Please do not tell me you are actually going to let the emotions you still have wrapped up in that dude cloud the plain picture right in front of you."

"Stop." Terry commanded calmly.

"Sorry! No! We have the opportunity of a lifetime sitting in the palm of my hands." He shook the papers he was holding. "And you better believe that I am not leaving it to chance on unresolved feelings."

"Anthony stop!" Terry stood up and faced him across her desk.

"No." That one word, though softly spoken, felt like a weight in her chest. They stood there opposite each other for several seconds. Terry searching for something powerful to say but coming up with nothing. She wavered. Not able to hold on to her resolve, she slowly lowered herself back to her seat and sat with her head in her hands. When she spoke again, her voice came out just above a whisper.

"Why won't you just let this go. I can handle this. I can handle Michael." Tears started to slowly slide down her cheeks.

Dammit. Anthony cursed to himself. I don't want to feel sorry for her right now. But he broke down and came around to sit on the edge of her desk and pulled her to him. "Hey. Come on. Don't do that. Come on. I know you can handle anything. But you are forgetting that you don't have to do it all on your own. And from the frustration you are feeling and the tears on your face right now, you need me. Or somebody, to help you get through this. Hey, look at me."

Terry resisted letting him pull her away from his side. It had been a long time since she was able to just wrap herself in her dad's arms and feel like the world could do her no harm. And for the first time in a long while, she felt that familiar comforting warmth and wanted to stay in Anthony's protective embrace. But to linger in this moment of peace was not an option. Anthony was determined to get her attention.

"Terry? Hey, look at me."

She didn't look up when she pulled away. She was a little embarrassed to have let herself show so much emotion. But Anthony understood.

"Hey. It's okay." He wiped the tears from her cheeks and lifted her face. "All I see right now is a strong woman fighting to keep her victory over her past hurt. And I know your tears are not a weakness. For you they are, kind of like a relief mechanism. So please, take a minute and let them flow. Because I cannot have you exploding all over my new shirt. I've only worn it once."

Making her laugh, Anthony successfully broke the solemn mood in the room.

"Your compassion is so overwhelming I just don't know how I ever survived without it." Terry responded sarcastically, wiping her cheeks.

"Thank you." He replied smugly to her sarcasm. Then he placed a light kiss on her forehead before rising from the desk to move away. Giving her a little space to gather herself.

She pulled out her compact and checked her face before turning her attention back to Anthony standing at the window. When she spoke, her voice was steady but carefully guarded. She didn't want to cry again when she shared with Anthony what he wanted to know.

"I,,, No. We were in love. At least that was what I believed. We lived together for almost a year. And one day it was all over. He had to go,,, be with someone else." Her next words had Anthony back at her side. "Man, what is wrong with me? Twice now. Two times Anthony. They, they just walked away to marry someone else. What? Why didn't I know? I ask all kinds of questions. I take my time. I am not so desperate to have a man that I would just ignore obvious signs. You remember Peter. He had almost everything going for him but, I dropped that fool so fast he didn't know what hit him. I don't, I don't..." She sat there shaking her head, trying to find words.

"Don't do that Terry. You are not responsible for another person's lies." Anthony spoke up.

"But I am responsible for seeing what is right in front of me. Ant, my job is to see past the obvious and to make others do the same. Michael, and now Reggie? I know the girls told you what went down on Saturday. And I really appreciate you not bringing it up. But it doesn't change the fact that I unknowingly walked into the wedding of the man I was supposedly working on a committed relationship with just days before. There is no way you can make sense of that. And us not having sex is NOT a legitimate reason for his wretchedness."

"First of all, your job is to make people see exactly what you want them to believe about your clients. That's our business and you are damned good at it. You know how it all works. That's also proof that there is nothing wrong with you. I know you. I know who you are and what you are about. We can do our best. But if a person is bent on hiding who they are, and you are not living with them day in and day out, it is entirely possible to miss what they don't want you to see. Heck even living with them, they can hide things. I don't know anything about your past with Michael so I can't comment on that. But I have been around during this thing with Reggie. You are not one of those women calling and checking on her man every hour. He took advantage of that. You can't make a man be honorable when that isn't who he is." Anthony explained.

"Yeah, that all sounds good, but.."

"But nothing." Anthony had to do something to stop her from blaming herself. Although he made sure he was upfront with anyone he dated, he knew both sides of being hurt. And for a moment he felt guilty. He couldn't let her stay where she was emotionally. "Look, it happened and now it's over. Dwelling on it is only going to keep your focus off of the rest of your life and the good you had and still have in it. You know who he is now. So now you have to let it and him go. Yeah, your feelings and your pride are hurt. But you sitting here beating yourself up is not going to change the fact that that motherf.."

"Anthony!"

"Look! I'm sorry! I'm just calling it like I see it. He didn't deserve you. And I'm glad as hell you didn't give it up." Anthony's anger was at a peak.

"Dude! Really?"

"I'm just saying." He turned to walk away, but had another thought and turned back. "And just so you know. You are too damned nice. Cause man, I would've set it off up in that church. That preacher would have had a wedding-funeral combo service. Two for the price of one." Anthony's declaration sparked a thought that made her start laughing. He looked at her with confusion. This was not funny.

"Ant, man! When I thought about it later, I was shocked that Leigh didn't bust back in there and turn over some pews. You know how she gets when it comes to her friends. Dude, I remember when that girl tried to flip out on you last year. She nearly set her weave on fire." As embarrassed as he was when it happened, Anthony couldn't help joining in on the laughter.

"Terry, for real, I thought I was going to be banned from my favorite restaurant."

She was so glad she had her friend to confide in. It wasn't easy letting him in to see her shame. But it was necessary and she knew she was in a safe space.

"Thanks Anthony."

"For what? This is what family is for. You can always talk to me. And I will always listen and do whatever I can for you. Even though you might not like what I have to say about it."

"Yeah, I know. Because sometimes you just do not know what to let come out of your mouth."

Anthony picked up on the return to their easy camaraderie and ran for the goal line. "Hey, I only say what needs to be said. You have to take that too if you want to continue to bask in the greatness of what is me."

All expression dropped from Terry's face. "Please tell me that you do not talk like that around the fellas. You don't, do you?"

Anthony's smile disappeared from his face and she could tell the wheels were turning and he was ready to spit out a comeback. But her friend refused the challenge, choosing to save it for another day.

"I'm going to let that slide. This time."

"Oooo, I'm so scared." Terry mocked a shudder.

"You need to be. Keep messing with me and I'm calling Leighann. You know I have my muscle on speed dial."

 "Whatever man. Get back to work and show me what you have on Evan. I just know that it is going to be a big deal."

"Yes it is. That's exactly what I was coming in to tell you earlier. Whatever this product is that Evan is working on, it is going to have a medical application that will have a major impact on healthcare. But his camp is being very closed mouth about this project."

"That's normal Anthony." Terry shrugged off his concern.

"No T, not this time. They are being much more careful than usual. I had to call in a major debt just to get general information about him meeting with several doctors over the last few months. And they told me that he's got a lot of money already tied up in this project. More than usual."

"Well, it looks like we have to go straight to the horse's mouth this time." Terry settled back in her seat to think.

"Looks that way. Let's do it. What's the plan?"

Terry sat silently for a moment before a smile spread across her lips. When she looked up and Anthony saw the fire in her eyes, he felt a calm come over him. Her fight has kicked in. She was going to be just fine. "She's back." He declared.

"You better believe it. Check this out." She pulled out her legal pad and started to write out her plan. They spent the rest of the afternoon, until around four, working on their strategy to move quickly but wisely toward the top of the list for this account. Gathering names and numbers and other information vital to their goal. Anthony went back to his office to send out emails and make phone calls, leaving Terry to her own devices.

Fifteen minutes before the end of the day, she took a brief break. Kayla followed her back into her office holding her schedule for the next day.

Terry took the paper and sat behind her desk to look it over. Midway through her review she remembered to let Kayla know about her instructions for Michael.

"Kayla, from now on, if I am out of the office, please just take a message or get Anthony for anything that Mr. Jacobs needs."

"Uh, okay. Is there something wrong?"

"No.   I just would rather not share any personal business unnecessarily. I'll be in later or please see Anthony is all we need to offer. Okay?" Terry didn't want to be too harsh with her instruction. So she kept her voice matter of factly.

"Will do. Are there any changes you need me to make to your schedule?"

"Mr. McGhee at 2:30? Who is this?" Terry questioned.

"He said you told him to call because he had some questions about a project he's working on. He did not leave his company's name."

"Hm. Ok. Well, I'll see tomorrow. And the conference call at 10:15? Who else will be on the call?"

"It's the usual, six total. No, seven. Mr. Jacobs will also be on the call." Kayla responded.

"Of course," Terry sighed. "Ok, looks fine. I will see you in the morning."

"Alright. Goodnight." Kayla turned to leave.

"Oh, Kayla."

"Yes ma'am."

"Anthony said he scheduled a meeting with Maria Henderson. Do you know what time?"

"Uh, just a sec." Kayla walked out to her desk to take a look at her computer. "It's 9:15 at her office."

"Ok. Thank you. Goodnight."

Terry locked her computer, grabbed her briefcase and left her office. Stopping to say goodnight to Anthony, she poked her head in his doorway. She waved bye when she saw him on the phone. But he waved her in.

"Mom guess who just walked in. Yes. Mom said hello."

"Hi Mom V."

"She said...., Ok. She heard you. Alright Mom, I'll call you later. Love you." Anthony hung up.

"How is she?" Terry loved her second mom.

"Good. Asking when I'll be coming to visit."

"And when the grandchildren are arriving as well?" Terry couldn't help throwing that in.

"Funny Terry. But no. She knows I'm not in any rush for that. So, are you heading straight home?"

"Yes big brother. Home, dinner, then bed. Does that meet with your approval sir?"

"Hey, don't shoot the messenger. I'm just following orders. Angela said to let her know when you were leaving and I intend to do just that. I'm not messing with her."

"Yeah, don't even try it." They both laughed at each other. "Alright, I'm out. See you in the morning. Oh, do you need anything for your meeting with Maria tomorrow?"

"No. I've got everything under control. Just keep your phone near just in case. But I'll have a good report when I get in." Anthony smiled confidently.

"No doubt. Night." Terry turned to leave.

"Night."

CHAPTER FIFTEEN

Traffic was a little heavier than usual, but it didn't make Terry's trip home too much longer. She always had an alternate route option.

Angela rung her doorbell about fifteen minutes after she walked into her house. She wasn't surprised though. Angela wouldn't be Angela if she didn't check up on her charge.

"Hi sweety. How are you feeling?" Angela hugged Terry, then pulled back to give her a once over.

"Actually, pretty good. A little tired still, but at peace for the most part."

"Good. What do you want for dinner? I'll whip something up before I head home." Angela walked past Terry towards the kitchen.

"You don't have to do that."

"I know that. But it would make me feel better to know you are actually eating well, as strongly suggested by Dr. Ryan." Angela gave her a look of warning.

"Ok, Ok. Do your thing Mother. I'll be right back."

Terry went upstairs to finish changing her clothes and came back down to keep Angela company while she made dinner. It didn't matter what it was, this chick could burn. And Terry's stomach was reacting to the wonderful aroma even before she could make it all the way down the stairs.

"Mmm. Smells so good in here. I didn't realize how hungry I was."

"Exactly. That's just how you got in this predicament. Now sit and have some tea."

Terry's eyes lit up. "Ahh yeah. Angela's famous tea. Taste so good you'd think you were drinking ghetto kool aid punch, laden with a splash of juice and darn near three cups of sugar." Terry chuckled at her outlandish description. "How do you do that without putting people into a sugar coma?"

"A secret I plan to take pretty close to the grave. It's one of the things that I control that make people do what I say. I just hypnotize them cup by cup." Angela bragged smugly.

Terry took a hefty swallow. "Lawd! I'm in a trance. What do you want me to do? I'll eat every bite you put on my plate and wash your car."

"I'll settle for a clean plate this time." Angela winked. Terry quickly nodded her agreement and sipped quietly on her tea while Angela finished cooking.

Terry wasted not a second diving into the plate Angela set before her. Chicken and shrimp scampi over pasta with steamed fresh broccoli was one of her favorites from Angela's kitchen. She had to have planned this meal because Terry knew she didn't have any shrimp or broccoli in her fridge.

"Angela, you take such good care of me. You are going to make a very special mother one day." Terry loved her friend so much that her heart skipped when she saw the light in Angela's face fade momentarily. She reached across the table and covered Angela's hand. "Hey. Sweety I'm sorry. I wasn't thinking."

"You're fine. It's been a long time now. And I'm ok." Angela brushed off her concern.

"Alright." Terry took a few more mouthfuls and decided that if she waited much longer, there was a good chance she would be in bigger trouble with her friend. All was quiet for the moment so this had to be a good time to break the news to her.

"Um, I want to let you know something." Terry started cautiously.

Angela's fork paused in mid air. "Do I need to brace myself?"

"Maybe a little."

Angela sighed, put her fork down on her plate and sat back in her chair. "Lay it on me."

"We got a new boss yesterday."

"Okay? So?"

"It's Michael." Terry whispered.

Angela tilted her head slightly and sat silently for several seconds before she spoke.

"Michael who?" She asked suspiciously. Terry decided to stop beating around the bush and lay it all out.

"You know who I'm referring to. They brought him in as the new Senior Manager - Media. We have talked a couple of times. Briefly. I will admit that it was a little tense at first."

"Oh no." Angela shook her head in dismay. "And I'm sure this had something to do with your going to the hospital. Didn't it?"

"It's ok. I was able to handle it. Anthony was there which took away some of the pressure. And today, I let Michael know in no uncertain terms that there won't be any contact or discussions that are personal in nature. I'm not going to pretend to be friends. And, Anthony has been brought somewhat up to speed and has my back on this."

Angela sat shaking her head, in a daze. "This cannot be happening. Wh.. what is going on? Reggie? Michael? You getting sick? Work and Car…" She stopped herself and took a deep breath and closed her eyes momentarily. "It's… It's like, like that thing they do in TV. Sweeps week, right? No, Rush Week in college. They send you through a week of near hell and drama just to prove what? I don't know. I didn't bother to do it. So I know there's probably more to it than just that. But they want you to, to…" Angela struggled to get out her thoughts. "I mean, everyday something big or crazy happening. I'm stressed out just thinking about all this! And it's happening to you, not me! I mean… Girl I don't know what I mean. Do you have any wine left over from the other day?" Angela needed to calm down.

"You know Leigh does not leave her alcohol behind." Terry was feeling sorry for her friend. Obviously there was something else going on that she was not sharing.

"I know. I just had to ask. Ok so, do you have any chocolate instead? That works just as well for me. Calms my nerves like you wouldn't believe." Angela laughed.

"Right! Let me take a look." Whew! That went so much better than she thought it would. Terry rose to see if she still had any chocolate left in her emergency stash.

"And get me the good stuff! I can get my own M&M's." Angela commanded as Terry disappeared from the kitchen. Terry poked her head back around the corner.

"Uh, beggars cannot be choosy."

Angela lowered her head, raised an eyebrow and calmly replied. "If you hope to ever taste another shrimp from my pan, you best move along and handle this chocolate business of ours." Both of Terry's brows shot up and her mouth fell open.

"You wouldn't."

"Try me." Angela crossed her arms and pursed her lips.

"Be right back." Terry skipped up the stairs to her room. Grabbing her Godiva stash, she also picked up the last two of her favorite Ferrero Rocher chocolates and headed quickly back downstairs. She allowed herself to keep only two handy because they were her weakness.

"Mother Angela!" Terry called out entering the kitchen bearing her gifts.

"Now that's what I'm talking about." Angela opened the box, grabbed a white chocolate raspberry chunk and bit into its richness. "Mmmm. Now that's good. I feel the endorphins rushing to my head already."

"Have as many as you like." Terry offered.

"Oh, I will."

Terry sat to finish her food. Angela always appeared steady and solidly secure. She was a rock for her friends. So it wasn't very often that Terry felt like she really did anything that Angela was truly in need of. She knew it wasn't necessarily the chocolate. But giving Angela that moment of peace and pleasure along with the simple action of doing something to help her take control of the emotions swirling within her was a big deal to Terry. Angela didn't shake easily. So Terry just gave her the time she needed to gather her thoughts.

"Thank you." Angela broke the silence.

"For what? You've been the one here for me."

"For understanding when I do need you. I know I hover. A lot." She laughed. "I know I act like I'm bulletproof. And you know that it's kind of difficult for me to be the one in need. So just, thank you. When all this stuff settles with you, we'll sit and talk. Ok?"

"You promise?" Terry would be patient. For now.

"Of course. Now, let's get down to the important question." Angela said, picking up her fork again.

"And what's that? "

"Is he still cute?" Angela popped a shrimp into her mouth. She was trying hard to stifle her laughter.

"Are you serious? I just can't with you!" Terry shook her head in disbelief.

Angela was laughing so hard tears started to fill her eyes. Boy, did she need this laughter.

"I couldn't resist. I'm sorry honey. But he was cute. And I was so hot with him when he messed up. Cause that Ricky boy you were seeing before him looked a little, uh, how should I say this, special." Angela couldn't stop laughing.

"You are cold blooded Angela. Ricky was just a friend that just kind of grew on me. We were never really serious and you know that." Terry protested.

"Yeah, I know. I was in prayer over that one."

 "What?"

"Yes ma'am." Suddenly serious, Angela confessed. "I was considering going on a fast just weeks before you told me you weren't going to hang out with him as much anymore."

Terry's mouth fell open. "You're kidding right?"

"Ok, I am. But you know what the old folks say. Be careful who you have babies with."

Terry couldn't keep her laughter in any longer.

"Ok, now I know you really do need to go on a consecration. You are talking way too much like Leighann right now. And we have got to shake that off of you."

"Girl, go get the oil!" They slapped a high five.

The lively conversation set the mood for the ladies to finish dinner, filling the room with laughter.

Angela helped Terry clean up and headed home a little after eight.

"Alright Lady, I'll talk with you tomorrow. Have a small glass of water before you turn in for the night." Angela instructed.

"Yes ma'am. Drive safe. And please, please say your prayers tonight. For me and for you. We don't need anymore of Leighann showing up unexpectedly. I don't think I can handle it."

"You? I Know I can't. Bye girl." Angela gave Terry a quick hug and kiss on the cheek.

"Good night." Terry closed and locked the door. She headed back to the kitchen to get some water. She took her time sipping her water as her mind replayed her very eventful day. "What a day," she declared as she grabbed a popsicle from the freezer, then snapped off the lights and headed upstairs.

"Bed. Mmm. I can't wait." she sighed, relieved that she could shut it down for the night. The clock read 8:32. "Perfect. Lord, let's catch up on this sleep. And while we're talking, I'm putting in my bid for a better, no, a great day tomorrow."

She stood in front of her bathroom mirror, looked herself in the eye and made a declaration. "And no matter what tomorrow holds, I know Father that you are who holds my future. I know that no weapon formed against me shall prosper. And whatever state I find myself in, in you Lord I will be content. That does not mean that I am settling for whatever life has decided to throw my way. But I can rest in you, knowing that you watch carefully over all that you have promised me, and all that you have said that I am and that I will be. And you have promised to make all these things that have come my way work for my good. You said that I would not be ashamed for trusting in you. And you cannot lie. So Daddy, I know you will get your glory out of this. And I will have joy and peace with the end that you expect and have prepared for me."

Terry finished getting ready for bed and grabbed her bible to read a little before closing her eyes for the night. By 9:10, Terry was sliding deep beneath her comforter. "Goodnight Lord. See you in the morning."

CHAPTER SIXTEEN
WEDNESDAY

Terry's morning began at it's normal pace with her usual Wednesday morning trek on the treadmill. Normally her routine was thirty minutes while she watched the news. But since she missed her walk on Monday because she went into the office so early, she did a full hour and then jumped in the shower.

She felt different. Calm, focused and centered. "Yeah God, today is going to be a good day." She declared as she slid into her car, waiting for the garage door to open.

Ten minutes to eight, she glanced down at her watch just before walking out of the elevator onto her floor. Kayla was just setting her purse down when she walked past. "Good morning."

"Good morning to you. I know you have a lot on your plate this morning so I will grab your coffee for you." Kayla offered.

"Thank you ma'am. Oh, did Anthony say if he was coming in before his 9:30 meeting?"

"Actually he was leaving the garage when I was pulling in." Kayla reported.

Terry smiled from ear to ear. "Now that is what I call dedicated, dependable and my favorite partner in crime. That dude is about business. Thanks Kayla."

"No problem." Kayla left to complete her small errand.

Terry settled in at her desk and got down to work. Minutes later Kayla walked in, sat down her favorite coffee mug and left the room without a word.

Her daily routine machine was up and running smoothly. No smoke or rattle. "Yes, this is going to be a good day," she whispered over the rim of her mug.

She was so engrossed in her research that she didn't realize how much time had gone by until Anthony walked through her office door.

"Hey."

"Hey An..." Her voice immediately caught in her throat. As soon as she saw the sternness of his face, a knot dropped into the pit of her stomach. She looked at the clock on the wall and frowned. 9:43 am.

"What happened? You're back way too soon."

"Yeah. Well. Maria saw me earlier than scheduled but she didn't really have much to offer. Evan isn't using any of his previous resources. I don't get it. Instincts are to begin with what you know and what's already worked for you. But he's completely changed his M.O. Which leads me to believe he is not heading this project alone. We've got an unknown player." Anthony's concern was unmistakable.

"Ok, then. We'll keep working on that. Now, what is the real problem?" Terry knew Anthony too well to not know that there was more.

Anthony stood contemplating his next words. This really made her stomach do a flip. He was never at a loss for words.

"Ant, what is it? Look, don't drag this out. Just say it." Terry ordered.

"It's Tadashi."

Terry took a deep breath.

"Okay." Terry sat her pen down and pressed her back into her seat to brace herself. "What have you found out? "

"My sources have informed me that Cameron Robertson has yet to return stateside. That he's been in Tokyo all this time. He's spent as much time as allowed in Tadashi's offices there." He glanced at his watch. "It's almost midnight there now. I spoke to Karen here in their Georgia office on my drive back here. And all she would tell me is that their Japan office has expressed a contract to her that she will receive by tomorrow. Once she reviews the package, she will call the parties involved in the negotiations and arrange to have the signed contract delivered some time tomorrow afternoon." Anthony finished and stood waiting for her response.

"The parties involved?" Was all Terry asked.

"That's all she would give me."

"That's all?" Terry asked again in disbelief.

"Yeah." Anthony's frustration was now coming through loud and clear,

"Hmm. Well, I guess we know what that means." Terry sighed softly, slowly shaking her head. She took a deep steadying breath to try to slow her pounding heart before opening her eyes again. Anthony was now standing quietly by the window. She rose from her seat and walked to stand beside him, looking out of the window.

"That was the one." Terry said, talking to to herself as much as she was to Anthony,

"Yeah, I know. But it's not over until we get that call." Anthony wasn't one to give up easily. "Let's not write it off just yet."

"Man, the paper is signed already. So, at this point, it is what it is. We worked our butts off on this account and I am trying really hard not to get angry right now." She stood in silence for a moment, taking in the view of the city before she turned to go back to her desk. I have to be positive, she thought to herself. "Alright. We'll wait for the call. But in the meantime, we need to get on this Evan Blake matter. Oh, and do we have a meeting set with Boston yet?"

"As a matter of fact, I spoke with them yesterday before I left. I usually hear from them within 48 hours, so we should have a funds transfer scheduled by tomorrow." Anthony predicted.

"You're very confident."

"I'm very smart. And we're extremely good at what we do. What we put together will be like gold to them and they know it. Our last campaign increased their sales double digits the very first week. They'll pay."

"Such a shark." Terry teased proudly.

"And don't you forget it." Anthony winked and retrieved his briefcase to leave. "I'll talk to you in a few. I've got a few phone calls to make."

"Ok. It's about time for the morning call anyway." Terry sighed.

"Oh, I really have to go now."

"Run Forrest Run!" She laughed at his retreat.

The morning passed as scheduled. Terry thought Michael did well leading his section of the call. Though she'd never tell him so. That would only encourage him to cross the boundary line she put in place.

Just as Anthony predicted, right before lunch she received the call from the Boston account to confirm acceptance and payment. She picked up her phone and dialed Anthony's extension to let him know but he walked in before she could leave a message.

"Hey, I was just calling you." Terry said, dropping her phone back into its cradle.

"Yeah? You inviting me to lunch? Because I already have plans." Anthony responded.

"Ha! I know better than that. If you don't bring it up, I don't even bother. I was just letting you know that the check's in the mail. So we can scratch Boston off the list."

"Exactly." Anthony replied smugly, plopping down in the seat in front of Terry's desk.

"Whatever man. What did you need?" Terry brushed off his smug response.

"Testy. Anyway, I've got a call in to Gail Bradshaw."

"That name sounds familiar."

"I introduced her to you about six months ago in Dallas." Anthony's face brightened with a small smile.

"Ah yes. I remember now. Tall, bronzed, blonde Latina woman with the great...smile."

"Yes, Exactly." The smile on his face was deceptively innocent but didn't hide the glint in his eyes. Terry had a hard time holding back her laughter.

"Ahem. So, what exactly are you waiting to hear from Ms. Bradshaw about? That would concern me, of course." Terry carefully asked.

"I had an epiphany." Anthony thoughtfully responded.

"Epiphany? Or a flashback?" Terry joked.

Ignoring her interruption, he continued. "And I suddenly remembered part of the conversation we had while we were together that evening." He sat forward in his seat. "She's very well connected with the medical research sector. Pharmaceuticals mainly. But I have a feeling that she may be able to assist us with our new research project."

"Oh really?" Now sitting up in her seat she declared, "Her smile just got a lot brighter."

"Exactly." Anthony gave a wink in agreement.

"What's with you today and all your exactly's?" Terry quizzed.

He just chuckled and rose to leave.

"Oh no, I think I've just entered the ego boost zone." Terry had to be careful with her words around him when he was on one of his ego trips. Although they were fun to watch.

"What on earth do you mean?" Anthony asked innocently.

"Anthony. Boy, just go to….lunch. You are so bad."

"That's just your opinion. But I'll confirm your hypothesis after lunch." He winked and turned to leave.

"Get out, please." Terry playfully shooed him away. "Ah! What am I going to do with you?"

Unexpected, when he turned around to respond, Anthony wore a sober expression and his eyes were very intense. But more surprising, was his response.

"Just pray. I'll be fine. See you after lunch." He turned to walk out.

"Hey!"

"Yeah?" He stopped his exit to face her again.

"Everything will work out. And I'll be fine. We'll both be okay. You know that right?" Terry surprisingly needed to reassure him.

"I know. Because I'll take care of you." Anthony said confidently.

"Anthony, you don't have worry."

"No I don't. Because I'll handle it." He spun around to leave and tossed over his shoulder, "We'll talk again after lunch. I may take a few extra minutes today." With that, he disappeared through the doorway.

Terry sat for a several minutes thinking about Anthony's mood. For the first time since her ordeals began this week, his worry showed through. He always had a lot to say about anything concerning her, but he never allowed himself to show too much emotion when doing so. But then again, maybe there was something else going on with him or his mom on top of everything happening here at the office. It was probably time that she made one of her check in calls to Victouria. Anthony wouldn't load anything else on her plate right now. But by calling directly to Mom V., she'd be able to find out if there was anything going on with them that she needed to know about.

"Thank you Father for my big brother. I didn't realize how worried he was about everything going on." After a moment, a smile spread across her face. "Well Lord, you know I've been working on him. And miraculously, he did say to pray. So, let's give him something big to give you thanks for." She got up from her desk, trying to hold back a fit of laughter while on her way to grab something from the building's cafeteria. "And I don't mean 'lunch" either." God has got to have a great sense of humor she thought.

CHAPTER SEVENTEEN

She worked through her lunchtime, munching on her chicken sandwich and vegetables. Kayla's return to her own desk was Terry's signal to finish up what she was working on and get ready for her next meeting. Today was one of those times when she didn't have a clue what she would be discussing. And anytime that happened, she liked to come to a definite stopping point in her workflow to make sure she wasn't distracted by anything on her desk.

Terry was staging samples of her work for easy access anytime during the meeting when Kayla walked in with her appointment.

"Terry, Mr. McGhee is here."

"Great." She rose to greet her guest. But the face she saw when she looked up startled her.

"Dr. Ryan?"

"Good afternoon Terry. How are you?"

"I'm doing well. Or so I thought. With you here, I'm not so sure now. And add to that, I'm a little confused at the moment. You are Dr. Ryan, right?"

"Dr. Ryan McGhee at your service." His smile lit up the room. He has got to stop doing that, she thought distractedly.

"Now, how could I have missed that?"

"Don't be too hard on yourself. You had a lot going on yesterday. It's understandable if you forgot most of what everyone had to say to you." Dr. Ryan explained.

"Well, um...please, please have a seat." Shake it off girl. Keep it together. "So, tell me. Is everything alright? With me? It must be something.... No...." She stopped her words and smiled nervously, trying to regain her composure. This doctor came all the way to her office. And for what? Dear Lord what is going on?

"Terry, please do not be alarmed. I'm not here to see you regarding your health."

"What? You're not? I don't understand."

"No. I'm sorry. I must not have been clear enough when I made the appointment. I'm here to talk about this project that I am involved with. Actually, I'm more than just involved. I'm the creator."

"Ah. That's right. It's coming back to me now. You did say you wanted to run something by me. That definitely puts my mind at ease." She visibly relaxed in her seat.

"Good. I apologize for worrying you. I'd hate to begin our relationship by being a source of pain or stress for you." His compassionate words could have become something more personal to her than just that if she wasn't fighting like crazy to ignore the look she thought she caught in his eyes. And the way the tone in his voice suddenly changed had her senses at full attention.

Terry's stomach did a quick flip. She swallowed hard and looked away to the samples sitting on the side of her desk. She did a quick self check. What is happening here? I barely know this man. Keep your mind on business. That is the only reason he is here.

"Thank you Dr. Ryan. You're fine. Now, let's see how I can assist you."

"Well, first of all, before we talk I need to give you this to review." He handed her a sheet of paper. "I'm sure in your line of business you are more than familiar with non-disclosure agreements. This is my first major venture so I'm still learning the process."

"Yes, of course. Just give me a moment to look this over." Her serious business radar went up a notch. Non-disclosure? This is going to be interesting. She took a minute to read the paper in her hand.

Terry took her pen and signed her name, then handed the form to Dr. Ryan for his signature before she slid it into her scanner. "Now, if you'll give me a moment to scan this into my system, I'll start your file." Normally she would have Kayla handle things like this so she could continue with her consultation. But the good doctor's presence was again throwing her, it seemed, off balance. She felt like she needed another minute before she turned back to face those eyes.

She ran the sheet through her scanner and quickly entered some additional information into her computer and then turned back to her guest.

"Alright Dr. Ryan, here is your original. Now, are we ready to proceed?"

"Yes. Here is what we've put together so far for inclusion in our press packet. And for you, there are a few extra documents with details on the apparatus I've designed." He passed the folder to Terry and waited quietly while she looked through the contents.

Halfway through her review, Kayla came in and handed a packet to Dr. Ryan. "This is for you Dr. McGhee."

"Thank you Kayla. Dr. Ryan, uh Dr. McGhee..."

"Dr. Ryan is fine. Please, both of you." Kayla nodded her agreement and left Terry to carry on.

"Alright. Dr Ryan. This packet contains some basic information about our firm, its services, and important contact information. There are also some things listed that you should consider when choosing an agency to handle your media presence. Please take this time to go through it while I finish looking through your materials."

"Sure. Please Terry, take your time. I know it's a lot of information." Terry nodded and quickly turned her attention back to the media packet.

She was so engrossed in the materials she was reading, she didn't notice how closely she was being observed. Likewise for Dr. Ryan while watching her reactions and each change to her expression. He was so focused on her that he didn't notice the soft smile that had formed on his own lips while staring at hers. Was he simply pleased because she appeared to like what she was reading? When she looked up from the folder, he had his answer. There was more. But business first.

"Well Dr. Ryan, this is pretty fascinating. And I can't say that I've seen or heard of anything quite like this."

"I am very glad to hear that. We've gone to great lengths to keep that as the case during our research and trials."

"So, tell me, at this point, what are you looking for from us? Once you give me the scope of your needs and vision, I can prepare a proposal for you to review during your selection process."

"To be honest with you, I already believe you are the agency we need to work with on this. And you, specifically."

"Really? Well that sounds great. But I do need to ask. Have you talked with anyone else about this?"

"No. No need." He quickly declared. There's that smile again. Stay focused, she reminded herself for what seemed like the the tenth time since he entered the room. He continued.

"I've spent a great deal of time reviewing the track records, reputations, and cost effectiveness of several agencies around the country. You and one other firm were at the top of my list. And imagine my surprise when the name Terry Ellis appeared at the top of the chart of one of my patients."

"What? So you knew who I was yesterday?" Terry asked with a little apprehension.

"Terry is a common enough name that you simply cannot assume you know someone by what's on a piece of paper. Only after I asked about your profession was I sure."

She sat silent for a moment to weigh his words. Replaying her brief hospital stay in her mind, she did remember that they were pretty far into her visit before he asked what she did. She relaxed again.

"Alright. Fair enough."

"So are you saying you'll take on my account?" He asked, with expectation in his eyes.

"Well, I think our next step is to prepare our proposal for review by you and your partners."

"Listen. I'm going to cut straight to the point. I don't believe you just ended up in my E.R. by accident. Everything I've done with this project has happened in a way I could never have planned myself. Your name was at the top of my list to work with. Your work is exemplary. And your reputation and accomplishments fit well with the credibility and vision I have for this product. I need to know that I can trust the agency and individual who represents me to push us ethically first, and for profit second. Everyone I've spoken to, and everything

I've read tells me you are the person I need to have on my side. So prepare whatever you need and send it here." He pulled out a card, and wrote an email address on the back. "We can work out any details we need to adjust or revise once I receive the documentation. I'll also want to introduce you to my partner as soon as possible. Once I speak with him, I'll contact you." He sat back in his seat and crossed his arms with a satisfied grin on his face.

"Well." Was all she could say. She looked down at the card and then back at him. No questions, scrutiny or cost haggling. This was definitely a different kind of experience.

"Dr. Ryan, are you certain you are ready to move forward with our firm?"

His answer was simple. He opened the folder Kayla had given him and pulled out the form that states the intent to hire the agency. He had already filled out and signed it while Terry was reviewing his product information. He slid the signed document across the desk in front of her. A small laugh escaped her lips.

"Alright. It looks like we are in business. Just keep in mind that, according to our terms of service, either party may cancel this agreement at any time and for any reason. If that occurs, all materials received from you that contain specific information about your product will be returned to you within 72 business hours. We will maintain rights and ownership of any materials that have been created by this agency and its employees that have not already been delivered as finalized and purchased. References to your specific product information will remain protected as outlined in our contract. Any outstanding billing for work completed, and man hours billed up to the date of cancellation must be settled within 30 days of the contract cancellation. The remaining provisions are listed in the packet you now hold and in any future amendments we agree upon. I like to make sure my clients understand that their intellectual property, and ours, will be protected at all times."

"Understood.   This process has been a huge eye opening experience."

"I can imagine," Terry sympathized.

"Well, Terry, I will call you as soon as I hear from my partner. And I'll be on the lookout for your email."

He rose from his seat and for the first time she noticed what he was wearing. Certainly, scrubs did not do this man justice. She shook off her thoughts and rose to take his outstretched hand.

"Dr. Ryan, it was a pleasure to see you again and under better circumstances."

"It has truly been my pleasure. I'm getting excited just thinking about the prospects of what's about to happen next."

Did he have to say that while still holding my hand and smiling like that?

"I hear you. Creating is an exciting process. I think that's why I enjoy it so much. I'll be in touch." She gently pulled her hand away.

"Great. Have a wonderful afternoon Terry. Take care." Dr. Ryan said his final goodbye.

"You too. Bye now." He turned, grabbed his briefcase from the floor and walked towards the door. And she missed not one motion. When he reached the door he turned briefly, still smiling, and nodded towards her before continuing with his exit.

Terry sat down and played the meeting back in her head. She sighed deeply and whispered a prayer. "Dear Lord, you already know. My emotions have been all over the place lately. So I am really going to need your help to keep it together." With a laugh, she continued, "Yes, yes. Every good and perfect gift comes from you. Thank ya.

Cause that right there, is pretty darned close. Smart, compassionate, accomplished and fine.   Woo Lord, I need to pray.   Wait, I am praying." Laughing at herself, she turned the folder face down on the corner of her desk and went to talk to Kayla. "I have got to get focused," she told herself.

"Kayla, check Anthony's schedule and give me a block this afternoon. I see his call light is still lit on the phone. Whenever he gets free is fine."

"Alright."

Terry headed to the restroom just so she wouldn't have to go right back into her office and to her own thoughts. She needed a few minutes to clear her mind. Unfortunately for her, the timing of her return trek down the hallway placed her directly in Michael's path.

"Ugh. I do not need this right now," she whispered.

"Good afternoon Terry."

"Good afternoon." She gave a small nod and kept it moving.

"Terry?" Michael wasn't going to let her just pass by. She stopped, pasted a neutral expression on her face and turned back to him.

"Yes?"

"Hi."

"Good afternoon," she repeated to say we've already spoken.

"How are you doing today?"

She took a deep breath, clasped her hands together in front of her, and smiled professionally.

"We're doing great today. Business is going very well. Both a check and a new client today. So, the machine is firing on all cylinders. Thank you for asking. You have a good afternoon." She nodded politely, turned and walked away. She hoped he would not stop her again. And he didn't.

Michael did contemplate stopping her but decided against it. It's only been a couple of days since he'd walked back into her world. He didn't want to completely alienate her before he had the chance to tell her what was on his heart. Take it slow. There will be other opportunities to talk to her. He didn't know exactly what to hope for. But there had to be a way to eventually set the stage so she would at least hear his apology. Whether she accepted it or not. He had to try. Today was just not that day.

CHAPTER EIGHTEEN

Instead of going straight to her office and risk dwelling on her run in with Michael, Terry headed to Anthony's to update him on their new client. She poked her head in his doorway to find him still on the phone in an intense conversation. She decided not to wait and come back later. But just before she turned away, his face changed suddenly from intense to anger. The tone of his next words was ominous. "What did you just say?....That son of a..." Now she couldn't leave. She moved until she was standing fully in the doorway, catching his attention. But what she did not expect to see was the look of annoyance that crossed his face when he looked up and saw her standing there. Her fight instinct immediately kicked in. She took her "I'll wait" stance and firmly stood her ground to wait for him to either end or include her in his conversation. Either way, she wasn't leaving. And knowing his partner, he simply motioned for her to come further into the room. She did him one better and perched herself on the edge of his desk. He looked up at her, then over to the chair in front of his desk, and then back to her. She smiled sweetly, crossed her arms across her chest and waited. Anthony just gave in and turned his attention back to his phone call.

"Well, has he been able to get in to see him?" He focused his attention back to his call.

"So, as of last night, no?" Anthony grabbed his water bottle and took a gulp, pausing to think for a moment.

"Alright Gail. Thanks for everything. I'll call you later this week. Bye." Before the phone reached its cradle, she started the inquiry.

"So? What was that all about? Especially since I could tell you really didn't want me to hear it?"

"That damned Cameron."

"Ah, come on. We already know he's trying to take the deal with Tadashi. Ant, we've done all we can at this point." She stood to walk around and sit in the seat he offered just minutes before.

"It's not Tadashi. It's Blake."

She stopped in her tracks. "Blake? Blake who? Not our Blake?"

"Yes."

"No! Not our Blake! God, what the heck is going on? Ahh!" She shook her fists in front of her and then plopped down in the chair. She sat there for a moment shaking her head, trying to keep calm. "That snake in the grass. First Tadashi and now he goes after Blake. And Anthony, if he managed to take the Tadashi contract from under us, he lied. That's the only way he can beat us. He's never provided better services than we have. So I know that he sold all kinds of promises he cannot keep himself. It's like clockwork. He hits his creative brick wall and then farms out his problems for others to pick up the pieces. He causes headaches everywhere he goes."

"Yeah, I know. All too well." Anthony agreed.

"And just how did he know about Evan? I had to scrape to find out the bits and pieces I could. And we keep hitting a wall. Somebody, somewhere is talking. And we have got to find them." She stopped and turned back to Anthony. "So, that's why he left Japan in such a hurry and ran over to Europe. Isn't it?"

"Yes. But Gail said he hasn't been able to see Blake yet. She believes Blake was scheduled to return to the U.S. by tomorrow anyway. So Cameron really didn't have much of an opportunity to barge in on him. She's not 100%. But she's pretty sure the meeting schedule that she was aware of, wouldn't allow much time for that snake to slither in."

"Anthony, it's what snakes do. Find the holes." They fell silent. Both were in their own train of thought on what to do next when Kayla interrupted them.

"Excuse me, Terry."

"Yes?"

"There is a Mrs. Lewis here to see you." Terry didn't immediately catch the name at first. "She said it's about your car."

"Ah, Patrice Lewis. Send her in. Oh, wait, I'll talk to her in my office." She stood to leave but Anthony spoke up.

"Oh, no. You two can just talk here. That way I can give Angela a thorough report." Thankful for the interruption, he sat back in his seat with one of his mischievous grins resting on his lips. Terry just shook her head and gave in.

"We can talk in here Kayla. Thank you." Terry looked over to give Anthony a sarcastic smile before she turned back to greet Patrice as she entered.

"Good afternoon Patrice. How are you?" She extended her hand but Patrice bypassed it and wrapped her in a quick hug.

"I'm doing great. And you look to be as well." Patrice stood holding her hands, giving her the once over.

"I'm fine. Let me introduce you to my colleague. This is Anthony Broder."

"It's a pleasure to meet you. Angela told me you helped to move things along at the hospital." Anthony smiled in appreciation.

"Oh, I did nothing great. Really. It was the least that I could do to help." She turned back to Terry. "I just wanted to give you the update

I had on your car. And I thought, what better excuse could I have to stop by and check up on the patient myself. Have you been eating and hydrating?"

"Oh, yeah. I like her." Anthony broke in. Terry gave him a very specific eye roll and both he and Patrice laughed.

"Patrice I'm fine. And please, do not encourage him. My watch dogs are doing their job. Angela cooked for me and Anthony is trying his best to shield me from any drama. Even though it isn't working very well. I'm determined to keep it together."

"Good. Because your tone seemed a bit strained earlier. But you sound much better now."

"Earlier?"

"Well, your assistant was away and your office was empty when I first arrived. I had to wait outside a bit so I made a quick phone call. And don't worry, you weren't very loud. I only recognized your voice just before Kayla came back or I would have knocked to let you know I was here. But I have been doing this for a long time. And you don't have to hear, or even see every detail happening to know when someone's stress is running high."

"Well, rest assured. Anthony is doing his job."

"And very well, if I do say so myself. You'd be so proud of me."

"From the look on Terry's face, I'd have to say you are right," Patrice chuckled.

Terry butted in. "Please Patrice, I asked you not to encourage him."

"Oh, don't you worry Terry." Patrice turned back to Anthony and offered, "Angela has my number if you ever need it."

"Patrice!" Terry cried out.

"Sorry, Terry. Our patient's needs come first." Patrice gave her an innocent smile and then threw a wink Anthony's way.

"Oh, good grief. It's a conspiracy." Terry threw up her hands, surrendering in response to their laughter. "That's it, I'm taking this meeting to my own office."

"Great! Let's go. You have a better view anyway." Anthony chimed in. But Terry quickly stepped between him and Patrice to stop him from joining them. Fighting back his laughter, he taunted with fake innocence. "What? You don't need my help?"

"Oh no you don't. I've had about enough of you for one afternoon. Patrice and I will be just fine talking alone. Thank you very much."

"Are you sure you can handle her Patrice?" Anthony offered with mock concern.

"What do you mean mister? Patrice will be just fine." Terry quickly butted in. "Now, if you'll excuse us. And even if you won't. We're leaving now." Terry turned her back on Anthony to make a quick retreat before he could make more trouble.

"Have a good day Patrice!" Anthony called out through his laughter.

"It was wonderful meeting you. Until next time." Patrice was trying really hard not to laugh. But it was very difficult looking at the expressions on Terry's face.

"Patrice? Can we please leave now? Anthony, I will talk to you a little later." With that, she escorted Patrice next door to her office. Terry motioned her to take a seat on the small couch by the window while she pulled a chair from in front of the desk to face her.

"Now that we can focus, tell me what's going on." Terry offered her a bottle of water as she took her seat.

"Well, like I said, I came to check on you and to talk with you about your car. And I see Anthony certainly has things under control."

"Patrice, you don't know the half of it. But he's good at taking care of me when he needs to. He's that kind of dependable friend."

"So, how long have you two been friends?" Terry was curious about where that question was steering the conversation and she didn't want any misunderstandings.

"We've known each other since the year before I started working here. He and his mom kind of adopted me into their family. So rest assured, Anthony really looks after me as he would his sister."

Patrice smiled softly. "That's really good to know. And good to have someone like that in your corner. But what about your family?"

"My mom still lives in Charlotte. My dad passed away about six years ago. And I have a younger sister. She's 12 now." Patrice's brows lifted in surprise and Terry responded with her usual quip. "Yeah, she was a Surprise Anniversary Gift one year. She's a good kid and really smart."

"Well, I hope your mother hasn't been too worried about you. It looks like you are surrounded by great friends who go the extra mile for you."

"Actually, I haven't told her what's been going on." Terry confessed.

"What? You don't keep in touch with her?" Patrice asked.

"No, that's not it. We talk every one to two weeks. But with all that's been happening, I've been in the 'I'll call when things settle down' frame of mind. But things just kept happening."

"I can understand that. But, make sure you give her a call. You don't want your watchdogs to beat you to the punch."

"You are so right about that. Morgan Ellis is no joke when you're on her list. I'm calling her tonight." Terry laughed.

"Good. Now, to this car business. I've been told you didn't request a rental car while your Mercedes is out of commission. You have to have proper transportation available to you." Patrice shared her concern.

"Oh, that's because I already have another car and didn't see the need for the additional expense and trouble."

"Ok, well..." Patrice sat thinking. "Still, think about it. If you decide that you want access to a comparable vehicle, please tell me so that I can arrange to have one delivered to you immediately."

"Patrice, really. I'm fine. Thank you for the offer. The facility has emailed regular reports to my office on the repair progress, per your instructions. And I am getting around just fine."

"Alright. If you're sure."

"I am. Thank you. Now, was there anything else?" Terry asked.

"Actually, yes. I did happen to hear you mention something about Japan. Are you planning on traveling there anytime soon? I have close friends there and I think it would be good for you to meet them."

"Really? Well, I actually don't have any plans right now for a trip there. I had a client travel there at a critical time in contract negotiations. And, well, let's just say we're waiting to confirm the outcome right now." Terry responded, trying to remain positive.

"Ah. I see. But, if you do, please let me know so that I can arrange a meeting."

"I will. Thank you." Terry reconsidered her response. "Wait. You know what?" She shifted uncomfortably in her chair. "Listen. You don't have to do that. You don't owe me anything past the car repairs."

"I know. But my heart believes that you are a person that I want in our lives long term. Our paths are crossing in ways that are not simple happenstance. And although Jarod and I aren't that much older than you are, we've experienced enough to have learned that when God puts someone in our life and heart, the way He has placed you, you simply embrace them. And you pay attention to where and how you can be a blessing to their lives. You entering our lives, despite the way things happened, has been an incredible blessing to us. I'll forever be grateful. And Jarod, even more so. I don't think you truly understand the impact you have had on him. What he did could have caused you so much hurt. But when you looked at him, he saw compassion in your eyes. You weren't angry. Just being the person you are broke the hold that grief had on his heart." Patrice took Terry's hand in hers. "Terry, he's a changed man. And I know it's because of God's love in you." Patrice paused.

"Wow. That, that's really,,," Terry's voice trailed off and tears began to well up in her eyes. In her business, so much of her time with people is spent trying to discern how much of what a person presents to her is genuine or fabricated for public opinion. But she was already acutely aware of how different Patrice was from other people. Still, she was a little caught off guard by her words. The last person who gravitated to her like this turned out to be her guardian Angela. And true friends were hard to come by. She didn't feel like she had really done anything special but the sincerity in Patrice's eyes confirmed her heartfelt words. Terry also felt at peace sitting across from this woman. And there was a spark of anticipation about what her future would look like with these new people in it. When Terry looked up again, the message in her face was clear.

Patrice's smile broadened. "I believe that you understand what I am talking about. Like precious faith is so awesome when you encounter it. No matter the circumstances."

"Wow. I, uh, I didn't expect any of this." Terry rose from her seat to grab a tissue and dabbed at her eyes.

"Are you alright?"

"Yes. Yes I am. Don't mind my tears. My emotions have been all over the place this week." Terry came back and took her seat again. "It looks like I've gained another piece to my life puzzle."

"We both have." Patrice took her hands again. "I believe great things will come out of our meeting. And God works pretty quickly sometimes."

Terry nodded in agreement but was curious about her statement. "Sometimes." Patrice changed the subject before Terry could delve deeper into what she meant.

"Well, I am going to get out your way and let you get back to work. I believe I've taken up enough of your time." Patrice rose from her seat.

"You're fine. And despite your joining forces with Anthony, I'm enjoying your visit." Terry joked about her earlier distress.

With mock innocence Patrice replied, "I am so glad that I could help."

"Ok. Now I know I have to keep you two separated at all costs." Terry laughed and stood to escort Patrice out.

"You can run, but you can never hide." Patrice cheerfully threatened as she embraced her. "Have a lovely evening."

"I will." Terry smiled back.

"You'll be hearing from us soon. Take care." Patrice waved bye and headed for the elevator.

Terry started towards her desk and the folder from the meeting earlier caught her eye. She grabbed it and turned back to go to Anthony's office.

CHAPTER NINETEEN

"So, this is what I was coming to talk with you about earlier." She walked in holding up the folder.

"Ok. What is it?"

"Interesting is what it is. And innovative. I haven't seen anything like this before. And I believe it's going to be a great opportunity for us." She plopped the folder on his desk and planted herself in the seat in front of the him.

"Well, let's take a look." Anthony took the folder. And perusing the contents, tilted his head in interest.

"I know. Just imagine what we could do with this campaign." Terry said with excitement.

"Who else has seen this?"

"We are the only company they've approached. In fact, Dr. Ryan signed the intent letter before I could even finish looking through his information."

"Really? Without talking numbers with you first?" Anthony wondered.

"Apparently, the choice was made before the good doctor saw me at the hospital yesterday." Terry revealed.

"What?" Anthony dropped the folder on his desk. "At the hospital?

"Dude, this week has been so strange, I'm just going to roll with it." Terry responded with her hands lifted in the air.

"Pardon me. But uh, I am going to need a lot more information about this doctor character." Anthony wasn't convinced everything was alright.

"Don't go overboard. He was already planning to approach the agency about this. He said he was impressed with our reputation and track record. He also took it as a kind of confirmation that I ended up in the same emergency room where he worked." Terry explained.

"So you are saying he thinks that because you got sick, you are the one to handle his account. Really Terry?" Anthony countered in disbelief.

"Don't be so sarcastic. Look. I know you're still working on your perspective about divine intervention and a man's steps being ordered. But look at it like this. What better way to get a glimpse at a person's true character than when under pressure and facing a personal health crisis." Terry was not giving up.

"Ok. But still." He shook off her explanation.

"Anthony, look. He didn't put me in the hospital. My chart could very well have been picked up by another doctor. And, it could have happened in the afternoon when he wasn't even there. I'm the one who allowed myself to get so stressed out, and didn't eat right and take care of myself. I'm the one who allows myself to get so bent out of shape going to the dentist. Even though I've never had a bad experience with this doctor. And I won't see anyone else." She laughed at herself. Feeling a little embarrassed in front of Anthony, she continued.

"Man, I know enough Word, and have seen enough to know that all I have to do is remind myself and stand on the fact that I have not been given the spirit of fear, but of power, love and a sound mind. I know the inner power I possess and that my life is protected. If it's not my appointed time, my life is protected. I've faced riskier circumstances. And with confidence, just holding on to that fact. But I let that one thing break my guard down every time. That started it all. And even though I'm ten, no, a hundred times better about going, I still struggle in this area. I don't have to go through this upheaval of my peace. So beating this part of my past is a battle I will continue to fight until I win it. And Anthony, it is a fact that Dr. Ryan most definitely had nothing to do with any of the other things that happened to me over the past week." Terry finished what she had to say about the spiritual aspect of this week's events. She could tell he was getting uncomfortable.

"Look Terry…" Anthony butted in, trying to wave her off the subject. But she cut him off.

"Yeah. I went there. I listened to you. Now it's your turn to listen to me."

She knew how tender his heart really was. And it frustrated her how quickly he always closed his heart to anything she had to say about God and how His love showed up in their lives. Anthony was determined to hold on to his past hurt. But she was just as determined to love him through his hurt and the facade he put up everyday. So she softened her voice before she spoke again.

"Anthony, there is no way I could sit here with this kind of peacefulness, and calm after this kind of week without God's help. Man, I almost took myself out of here the last time I saw Michael. But I'm still sitting here. And I'm unmedicated." She laughed. Raising her hand to count off on her fingers, she continued, "After being shocked by Reggie's drama and lies, barely avoiding serious injury, then came the sudden shocking disruption of my stable work environment, and being rushed to the hospital fearing the worst… Ant, walking around with no medication is a miracle. And on top of that, that dude walks right back into my life, taking my promotion and putting me in a position where I have no choice but to see and talk to him. Man!" Terry sat shaking her head for a moment, fighting back tears. "Without God, I'd be sitting in a corner somewhere popping pills, downing a steady stream of alcohol, and wondering how long before it would all be over. It's one thing to have stuff happen along the way.

But back to back to back? You tell me. Who do you know that could handle all of this at once. And on their own. I'll tell you. No one."

They both sat silently. But for totally different reasons.

Anthony was battling within himself to hear her words through the cloud of his self imposed guilt and his anger at God. And it was a major struggle.   He still held himself partly responsible for Mikki's death. And why didn't God keep her alive? He just could not come to terms with not having an answer to that question. It affected every part of his life. Everyone tried to make him understand that the accident was not his fault. But he just couldn't find it in himself to forgive what he believed his selfishness caused and let the guilt go. He wasn't thinking of anyone else that night.   Just his own hurt feelings. So how in the world could God not hold him at least a little responsible for his only sister's death.

Because I love you. It's not your fault.

Anthony suddenly felt the sting of tears behind his eyes. He jumped up and turned his back toward Terry. That last thought couldn't be real. It just had to be his wishful thinking. He didn't want Terry to know she was getting to him. So he fiddled around with whatever was on the shelf in front of him until he felt the tears go away.

Terry was also digesting what she just said. It had been a very long time since she had spoken out loud about just how devastated she was when Michael left. The cloud of all the emotions of this week was suddenly sitting like a weight at the top of her chest. The recollection of those feelings was so strong. It would be so easy to let it float down into the pit of her stomach. Then maybe she'd have her excuse to take her emotional moment. Let everything go for just a little while and melt to the floor in a puddle of tears. Release a week's worth of pressure. It's work holding your head up through trials. And right now, she suddenly felt like she was facing the supreme court of trouble. The urge to cry became very intense. It was like just talking about it all gave the drama from the past week permission to take over.

The weight felt so heavy right now. Her mind started racing, trying to make sense of all these emotions. But what would happen to her? "Would I be able to let it go after shedding a few tears? How long would it take me, this time, to recover from the hurt and disappointment." She had to consider all that could happen if she let go right now. Then another thought suddenly stopped her emotional rollercoaster. "More importantly, how in the world could I sit here and crumble in front of Anthony after that speech I just gave. He'll never trust me. And I can't stand up for God bringing me through this mess and fall down at the same time. What the heck am I doing?" This time, when she opened her eyes, the tears that slid down her face were paired with a small smile.

"Wow," Terry said softly, looking over at Anthony.

"What? You have tears on your face and you're smiling. What are you smiling about?" He was truly perplexed.

"I was thinking about the words I was just able to say to you. I haven't talked about my past to anyone in years. And hearing it spoken really hit me hard just now. I, uh..." She paused to catch her breath. "I'm not broken." Another tear rolled down her cheek.

"Hey? Are you ok?" Anthony came around his desk and took the seat next to her.

"Yeah. It's just that I had this huge heavy feeling of sadness sitting right here." She tapped her chest with her closed fist. "And to be honest, I wasn't really sure if I was over him. And because of that, I've avoided the subject at all costs. You know, out of sight out of mind." She shrugged to shake off her embarrassment. "But, now I know. I'm not the same. I couldn't be. This time I bent, but I did not break. And just now, when I starting thinking about everything..., I saw it." She looked up at Anthony with amazement in her eyes. "For the first time I didn't just go through the motions. I actually recognized my personal test. My mind was ready to go through the motions. All of those crazy emotions. But the words... No, the Word that came out of me while I call myself trying to teach you something, turned right around and pulled me back from the edge. And I didn't drown in my feelings. I did not break."

By this time, she was talking to herself as much as to Anthony. No longer focused on him, she had risen and walked over to the window. Anthony was not quite ready to fully acknowledge where she attributed getting her strength. So he leaned back in his chair and took a moment to gather his thoughts before responding.

"You're a fighter. I told you the other day how I saw your strength. And it reminds me so much of Mikki. Over the years I've known and worked with you, you've handled everything I've seen thrown your way with such an amazing level of grace. Even angry. I mean, there were some days I wanted to straight kick ass. Uh, sorry. But you..." A smile of admiration formed on his lips and he sat forward. "You have this certain way of taking the dirt people dump in your lap and shoving it sweetly back down their throats. And you do it with a smile. You, my friend, are my hero." Anthony placed his hand across his chest in grand salute, making her laugh.

Surely, she made her point very plainly. She also noticed how Anthony redirected the credit to her success onto her. But there was no way to ignore her victory and how she achieved it. And she needed time to fully process her revelation as much as Anthony did. With Michael being around daily, she was confident that they would have a chance to talk about it again. There'd also be other opportunities to work on Anthony's heart. So she decided to go with the new course of conversation.

"We definitely have had some very special clients walk through those doors." She agreed shaking her head at the memories.

"Special isn't exactly the term I'd use. But I'll let you have the last word on that subject this time."

"Thank you sir. No need to add any more disputes to my day."

"Look, I'm sorry if I have been a little too hard nosed this week. You know I'd never intentionally do anything to hurt you." He did not like the thought of being the source of any kind of pain in her life. He was her self appointed protector. And that was unacceptable.

"Hey. Don't you dare try to take responsibility for any part of what's been going on. I know you love me. And I know you have my back." Terry took her seat again and faced him.

"I know. But Terry…"

"We've all had stuff happen to us. Some worse than others." She interrupted him. "Although you've given it your best effort, you cannot control the outcome of our business. And certainly not someone else's life. I really don't understand why so much has happened to me and why all at once. The only way to make sense of this is to believe that maybe it's been allowed into my life because I'm learning to lean on my help. My backup in Christ. And right now, that's all I've got. Your guess is as good as mine on the rest. But I can tell you this. All of this turmoil and drama somehow, someway, is going to work out for my good. I have to believe that. And I am going to stand on that. That God will get the glory out of this time in my life. And all that I ask of you, is that you don't ignore it when you see it. Okay?"

Anthony slowly nodded his head as a smile spread across his face. "See. I told you."

"What?" Wondering what he would say next, a frown creased her brow.

"You're good. Preached and put me in my place."

"Ah man!" Terry slapped his knee and laughed at him. "And don't you forget it." She stood up, accepting her victory gracefully.

Grabbing Dr. Ryan's folder, she waved it at him. "And this right here is like a shining star. The potential I can see in this project is very promising. I feel really good about it."

"So, once you get the materials scanned into the system, let me know. I only have one other matter that's pressing today. But tomorrow morning I can take a more detailed look at everything and we can talk about where you want to go with this." Anthony followed.

"Great! I'll have it scanned before I leave today. In fact, I think I'm going to get it done right away so I can slip out a few minutes early. It's been a long day, but I will not complain." Terry suddenly felt tired and stifled a yawn.

"Hey, you've earned it. Just make sure you say goodbye so that I can report your departure to General Angela. Oh, and tell Leigh that I did get her message but just haven't had a chance to call her back."

"Ok. Will do. Later."

Terry went back to her office and immediately began scanning the doctor's file so that she could leave as soon as possible. As she was saving the last bit of information, Kayla walked into her office. So close.

"I don't know what it is, but I'm about to be out of here. So I hope you can make it quick."

"I was just coming to tell you that Dr. Ryan called to meet with you again tomorrow." Kayla announced.

"Already?"

"He said 11:30 if you are available."

"That was fast. Looks like I'll be logging in from home tonight," Terry sighed.

"Alright. I'll put it on Anthony's calendar as well. Oh, and Kristine called to check on you while you were in with Anthony. She said to call her."

"Ok. Thank you. Anything else before I get out of here?"

"Nope. That's it. Have a good night."

"You too Kayla. Good night. And I'm out." Terry hit the power button on her monitor and rose from her seat, grabbing her purse in one swift motion. "I will see you in the morning."

Terry walked out of her office on Kayla's heels and headed to Anthony's office next door. Barely sticking her head in the door, she made her announcement. "Hey. I'm leaving. See you tomorrow. Bye." She turned to leave but Anthony called her.

"Terry!"

She stopped, took a deep breath and slowly turned back. "Yes?"

Anthony paused thoughtfully, for effect. "Have a good night dear." He smiled innocently.

"I'll get you for that. Just, not right now." She spun away and proceeded to the elevator. "Please let me get out of here without being stopped." She whispered.

Anthony laughed at her threat. But he did not delay in picking up his phone and texting Angela that Terry had just left. Now, unless there was another emergency, he was off duty for the night. He tossed around the idea of making a call for a dinner date, but thought better of it. He really needed to go over the material for Dr. McGhee's meeting tomorrow. It was barely enough time to have anything ready to present but he at least wanted to be able to talk intelligently and ask the right questions about the product.

CHAPTER TWENTY

Terry slid into her car and released a sigh of relief. Traffic had already started to get thick, but it didn't take her long to get to the grocery store. She quickly grabbed the three things she wanted specifically for the night. Butter Crunch Ice cream, Arizona Golden Bear Lemonade and a bag of peeled shrimp for tacos. Quick and easy was the plan for tonight. Her phone rang as she pulled into her garage and she answered without looking to see who it was.

"Hello Angela." Terry answered knowingly.

"Nope. Krystine. What you doing?"

"Oh, just got home. What's up?" Terry stepped into her kitchen and put her bags on the table. Then walked straight to the sink to wash her hands and ripped open the bag of shrimp to add water to quick thaw them.

"Just checking on you. I talked to Angela. She told me how you were still having issues at work and with your health. Girl what is going on with you?"

"I'm surprised I'm just hearing from you." Grabbing a knife, Terry proceeded to shred some cabbage and other veggies to make the slaw to put into her shrimp tacos.

"We just finished taping. You know how my time is when I'm filming. It's been so hectic trying to get these last days completed on time. I did see a text earlier in the week but thought maybe everything was ok since I didn't hear anything more from Angela. You know how detailed she is."

"Yes I do," Terry laughed. "I'm ok. It's nothing that I can't handle. My business and health issues are all under control. And I've got the perfect solution right here."

"And what, may I ask, is that?" Krystine asked apprehensively.

Terry flung open the freezer as if her friend could see inside. "Ice cream of course!" She laughed and proceeded to grab the other ingredients needed to complete her slaw from the fridge.

"You are so silly!" Krystine joined in with her laughter. "But I'll tell you what. This project is done and I've got a few weeks off. So you best believe as soon as I land, I'm hitting up a quart myself."

"I'll save you a corner."

"Uh Uh, I'm gone need about half." Krystine laughed.

"Wooo! Careful child. Your country is coming out. Hold on til you get on the plane, ma'am." Terry laughed. Krystine could easily be the most stuck up diva in the room. But when she let her hair down, all bets were off. "I feel a crab feast coming on."

"Girl, I've been keeping this body tight all summer. So, Saturday. My place. 2 o'clock. And bring some newspaper. It is on!"

"Got you Boo! I'll let Angela know. She'll probably be calling me ..." Terry's phone beeped. "Nope, she is calling me right now. I'm surprised she waited this long. Have a safe flight. See you Saturday, Love."

"OK. I'm glad you're better. Bye Hon." Terry switched over to answer Angela's call.

"Hello."

"What took you so long to answer? Were you still on with Krystine?" Angela fired off.

Terry frowned at her phone. "What makes you think it was her I was talking to?"

"We talked a little while ago and I figured she was going to call soon."

"Yes Mother, it was Krystine. And before you ask, I am making my dinner right now. I'm about to drop the shrimp for my tacos and I may decide there is extra if you want to stop by."

"May decide? And what is up with that?" Angela scolded.

"I am pretty hungry. It's not like someone left me anything for lunch or an afternoon snack" she laughed.

"Spoiled brat."

"You did it! So don't be mad at me." Terry flipped her shrimp into the pan with a mischievous smile.

"Dear Lord, what am I going to do with her?"

"Love me. Now are you stopping by or what?"

"I'll be ringing your doorbell in two minutes. Get my plate ready."

"Yes ma'am. The shrimp will be hot out of the pan when you walk in the door. See ya." She hung up and grabbed another plate for Angela who showed up right on time.

The front door opened and all Terry heard was "MMMM, MMMM!" from her guest. Angela had already stepped out of her shoes before she turned the corner. She washed her hands with a smile on her face. Terry's heart felt happy that her friend was already enjoying her efforts.

"Girl, I have a meeting before church begins tonight and I was debating on what to eat. And lo, and behold, Lord you put Terry's delicious shrimp tacos on her heart. And now here I sit, in the manifestation of your love for me and my stomach. Halle-Glory!" Angela threw up her hands.

"And I thought Krystine was the only one trying to win an Oscar." Terry laughed.

"Oh no child. Not trying to get any awards. Just shrimp. I'm so hungry. And I need something else to think about other than the day I've had. There is just way too much going on. I don't know if I'm coming or going today. So right now I am going to enjoy this meal, relax a little and get my mind together before my meeting."

Terry exchanged the prepared plate for the empty one in front of Angela and watched her inhale the food's aroma.

"Angela, what is going on with you. I know my life has been a stress for you but I can tell there is something else. What is it?"

Angela held up a finger to tell Terry to wait for her to swallow. "Girl, I am never disappointed when I have your shrimp tacos. Mmm."

"Angela. Don't change the subject. What is going on? I'm beginning to worry about you now." Terry took the seat across from her.

"Terry, please don't worry. Work has become hectic for a moment but it is nothing I can't handle. And besides, I told you we will talk about it later when things settled down with you. So don't you stress yourself. Because right now, all I am going to do is finish this good food right here."

"Alright. But that's all it better be." Terry bit into her own taco. "Mmm. You're right. My shrimp tacos are the best. Of course, your scampi takes the prize. Remember that next Thursday." Terry winked and took another bite.

"Such a self serving compliment. I know I taught you better." Angela replied between chews making Terry laugh.

"Mmm Hmm." Terry hummed with her mouth full. "Oh, and you will not believe who showed up at my office today."

"Should I actually know who?" Angela asked in doubt, taking another savory bite.

"Two words. Sexy MD." Terry responded with one raised brow and pursed lips.

Angela's lips stopped moving and her eyes grew big and round. "You're kidding me." But her surprise quickly changed to concern. "Wait. Why? Are you alright? An emergency doctor doesn't just show up for fun. What did he say Terry?"

"I'm fine. Okay?" Terry tried to reassure her.

"Are you sure?"

"Yes. Dr. Ryan came in for business. Remember when we gave him my card?" Angela nodded and Terry continued. "Well, it turns out that he was already considering hiring our firm. And then I show up there in his E.R., out of the blue."

"Wow. And I see you don't have any complaints about him not wasting any time using that number either." Angela said, eying Terry closely.

"Hush girl. I'm having enough of a challenge fighting my own wayward thoughts about that fine specimen of a man. I don't need you on my case, too. Just pray for me. You've seen him. Honey, the struggle is real."   Terry's confession sent the ladies into a fit of laughter.

They finished eating and Angela helped clean up.

"Ok. I've got to get out of here so I won't be late. Thank you again for dinner." Angela dried her hands, preparing to leave.

"You are very welcome. Anytime. Oh, and Krystine said crabs at her house on Saturday at 2 o'clock."

"Great! I'll let Leighann know. I owe her call tonight. See you later." Angela gave Terry a quick hug and kiss on the cheek.

"Bye Hon. Talk to you tomorrow." Terry followed Angela to the door where she quickly grabbed her purse, slipped on her shoes and walked out of the door with a wave.

CHAPTER TWENTY ONE

Just after six, Terry took her things upstairs, flipped on the tv and jumped into the shower. Afterwards, she wrapped her hair and grabbed her phone to check her messages before logging on to go over Dr. Ryan's materials. She saw the reminder to call her mother and immediately dialed her. No need to put it off any longer.

"Hi baby! I was just thinking about calling you." Morgan Ellis answered. "How are you? You've been on my mind a lot this week."

"Well why didn't you call me? I'm doing ok. How have you been?"

"I'm great. And I didn't call because I know how you get when I call before you do. You act like I'm checking up on you. So unless there is something urgent, I wait to hear from you."

"Ok Mom. I hear you. You don't have to wait. It would have been good to hear from you with the week I've had." Terry confessed.

"Oh? What's going on baby?" The concern in Morgan's voice was obvious.

"Don't panic. Please. I've had some challenges at work but things are working themselves out." Terry tried to put her mother's mind at ease.

"Working themselves out how?" Morgan asked softly. Terry heard her mother's true question but attempted to avoid fully answering it.

"Mom, look. You lose some deals and you gain some. You don't take it personal. You just keep pushing forward."

"So, that's all?" Morgan knew there was something more. Her daughter's descriptions were never this cryptic and void of detail. So she waited patiently for Terry's response.

"Ma…"

"Here it comes," Morgan cut her off. "What don't you want me to know? Let's see. If it was about your girlfriends, you wouldn't be able to hide your irritation. And you vaguely mentioned work but you haven't said anything about the man."

"Ma.."

"Ah! There it is again. You only "Ma" me when you don't want to tell me something. So, stop wasting our talk time and get down to the bottom of what's bothering you." Morgan put her foot down.

"Fine Mother. Acting like you know everything about me." Terry muttered the last thought but Morgan heard her.

"No, I do not know everything. But I do know you well enough to know that there is more that you need to tell me. So spill it missy."

"Oh, Alright. Here it goes. I hit a big snag with a major contract and I don't know for sure if I've lost it or not. That fool Cameron just won't go away. I wrecked my car. Reggie got married. And I ended up in the hospital dehydrated and stressed. But I'm better now. And I think I have a pretty good account that just made it to the books. So the trip to the E.R. actually paid off." Terry waited for a response. But there was only silence for what seemed like forever. "Hello?"

"I'm sorry. I think I may have blacked out for a moment. What the hell did you just say about Reggie?" Terry knew the exact look that was sitting on her mother's face at that moment.

"Ma'am?" Terry responded in surprise. Her mother never cursed.

"Girl, don't play with me right now. What did you just say?" The irritation was strong in Morgan's voice. Terry decided in that moment that she was definitely leaving out the part about Michael.

"He got married on Saturday. I had no idea. I felt stupid and angry. And it hit me really hard. The only good thing about it was that the girls were there and they took good care of me through it all. And right now, I am just trying not to focus on it because I have the rest of my life and business to take care of. And before you ask a bunch of questions, that's really all I have to say about it right now."

Terry stopped talking and waited patiently again for her mother to respond. But she was silent so long that Terry thought the call had dropped.

"Mom? Are you there?"

"Yes. I am definitely here." Morgan's voice was deceptively calm. "I just don't know what I could possibly say that would actually be constructive or helpful. Because, child, all I want to do right now is find that joker and string him up. And please know that once you've had some time to process this mess and get your emotions in check, we are going to have a very in depth discussion about this. That is non negotiable."

"Yes, ma'am." Terry simply agreed.

"And when were you at the hospital? Why the heck are you just now telling me about this? See. I've already told you about letting me know when important things like this happen. I bet Ms. Angela knows everything." Knowing Terry would protest her mentioning Angela, Morgan didn't give Terry a chance to speak. "Look here. I am your mother. You hear me. She can be your friend and all, but I gave birth to your behind. She's been there for you and I appreciate that. But don't make it hard for me to keep liking her." Morgan could not contain her irritation any longer.

"Ma!" Terry tried to interrupt her mother's rant.

"Don't you Ma me. You should have called me. I don't nose around in your life like some mothers. And all I've asked of you is that you give me a call at least once every couple of weeks so I know that you're okay. Of course I'd welcome more. I love to hear your voice. But I also know you have your own life with a hectic work schedule. I don't ask you for much. But I draw the line at my child being hospitalized for any period of time and no one tells me about it!"

"Mom, I'm sorry! Please calm down."

"I am calm!" Morgan yelled.

"Is that so? Because I really can't tell." Terry tried laughing the tension away but it did not work.

"Are you making fun of me now?" Morgan asked with warning.

"No ma'am." The smile disappeared from Terry's face. "I just don't want you to be mad. Mom I'm sorry. I really am. There's been so much going on. And I've just been trying to catch my breath. It was like before I could process one thing, something else happened. You know I'm not a big complainer. And I try to handle whatever happens myself. But Mom, this week has both flown by and dragged along at the same time. And today I realized that I hadn't talked to you since the drama started. It wasn't on purpose. So charge it to my head and not my heart. Please."

"Mm hm. Alright." She hated tension between her and her daughter so she easily accepted her apology. "But next time I'm getting on a plane."

"Bring it on Dr. Mae." Terry called Morgan by the nickname she gave her years ago when she received her Doctorate. However, Dr. Morgan Alexa Ellis did not care for it at all.

"See. You were forgiven and now you're about to go right back into the doghouse. That is not my name."

"Mommy, you are such a city girl." Terry joked.

"Mommy? Don't try to sweet talk me now. And yes I am." Morgan proudly admitted. Terry laughed at her mother.

"Alright city girl. I need to review some material for tomorrow."

"Ok baby. I'm so glad you finally called." Morgan's motherly tone returned and struck a nerve in Terry. All of a sudden she wasn't ready to hang up.

"Mom?"

"Yes baby."

"Nothing. I'll talk to you soon." Terry changed her mind.

"Baby, what is it?" She waited this long to call her, Morgan wasn't going to hang up until Terry said everything she needed to.

"I just.. I just wanted to ask how do you do it?"

"Do what honey?" Morgan wondered where this conversation was headed. But whatever came next, her heart was open to her daughter.

"How do you stay so strong? I mean, I know you are in a good place right now. And we've had a pretty good life. But I also know that you've gone through some pretty hard times. Dealing with us, the extended family issues affecting our family, school, and especially with Dad. He definitely had a lot of great moments with us. But God knows, there were times that even made me think twice about getting married." Terry laughed. "He could be a piece of work. But I know he loved us. And most of the time you seemed so in love with him. But when we lost him, it was like you somehow got even stronger. I want to know how? How in the world do you keep it so together?"

Morgan released a huge sigh. "That is such a loaded question sweetheart. And I must have done something right for you to think that I've done so well with my life. But I have to be honest with you honey. It took me a long time to get to where I am now. And trust me, it took your father to hold me down a couple of times when your aunt on his side was going through her mess. You know I do not play when it comes to other people's foolishness affecting my kids. We sent you next door a lot during that time so you wouldn't see the drama. But I almost choked the mess out of her one time. She brought some mess in my house and I lost it."

"Mommy, you didn't?" Terry asked in disbelief.

"Child! God really wasn't through with me back then." Morgan laughed.

"It's a wonder that I didn't get to see more of that Morgan fire. I thought dad was the only one."

"Oh, your Dad and I had many behind closed doors discussions. And almost just as many we're going to take a drive, be right back moments. Both together and just to get away from each other." Morgan laughed to herself at the memories of some of the stupid fights she and Eric had.

"So that's what was going on?"

"What?" Morgan asked cautiously.

"Mom, there was one time I seriously thought you two just didn't like me," Terry revealed.

"Huh?" That surprised Morgan.

"Yeah. It felt like you were always mad at me. For a while, I was miserable. And I just could not figure out what I had done. All I knew was when I walked in the room, you would stop talking and one or both of you would leave the room. And sometimes the house." Terry explained.

"Oh baby. I remember. I knew you could feel the tension. But I had no idea you thought it was because of you. I am so sorry." Terry could hear the emotion in Morgan's voice.

"Mom, please don't cry. It's alright. Things got better and I got over it. And now I have a better understanding." Terry reassured her mother.

"Yes. But still. I wish I had handled things better. But when you know better, you do better. And it was journey for us. Our family had some very trying times. And then add to it the stuff coming at us from my work, and our private business. Child, there were days I'd just take a half day of vacation, leave work and go park somewhere to cry until I had no tears left." Morgan revealed. "Then I'd come home, make dinner and check on homework or whatever was needed. Praying all the while that I would make it through the night. It was not easy. But I knew I couldn't give up. I had you to be strong for."

"Wow. I know our family had it's issues. But I had no clue that you were having such a hard time." Terry had a new level of compassion for her mother.

"Good. It's a parent's nightmare to have their children living wrapped up in their confusion. I am just so sorry that you had to deal with any of our mess at all. And that I did not see your pain from all the tension in the house." Morgan apologized again.

"Well, you didn't directly say anything about it. But I thought you finally understood how I felt and tried to fix it."

"Really?" Morgan's curiosity was piqued.

"Yes ma'am."

"Why?" Thinking back to that time, Morgan was putting two and two together and getting a pretty good idea where she got this belief from. But she decided to let Terry tell her what made such an impression on her, rather than risk haphazardly confirming something that she didn't already know.

"Well, dad always traveled a lot with work. But this particular time, we spent so much more time together while he was away. You even let me sleep with you for a few nights. And it had been years since you let me stay the whole night in your room. I was in pillowtop heaven." She laughed. "You know, I still have the receipt from our trip to the spa and the two pictures we took that afternoon. I really felt like I got my mom back that day. I knew that whatever I had done was forgiven. You loved me again."

"Oh baby. I had no idea. Maybe because I was so blinded by my own feelings. Honey, those days were very special because I truly needed that time with you. Your smile and hugs were like a medicine to me. It was such a good time for us. But it was also a little bittersweet." Morgan decided that it was time to tell Terry the truth.

"Why?" Even though it was a long time ago, she wasn't sure she wanted to hear the answer. But she had to ask.

"Why? Because that time he wasn't away on business. Your dad and I had decided to separate. And he rented a place across town and worked from there."

"What? Are you kidding me?"

"No honey. And your father isn't here to defend or explain himself. So all I'm going to say about it is that there was no infidelity involved. We simply had very different expectations of what marriage was. We had very different examples growing up and no tools to reconcile what we knew into a single fluid picture that was just ours. Unique to our family unit. Don't get me wrong. No relationship is perfect. And it's unreasonable to expect it to be. But you do want the best for your life. And when your views are so different, it takes a great deal of work to make a marriage survive. You have to come together and figure out what is best for the family you now have."

"So, how did you fix things?"

"Well, I can't speak for him. But I was just over everything that had built up. We were dealing with the past showing up in our present, no longer feeling heard or valued, the constant dissension, and the loss of our closeness and intimacy. Everything just felt broken. I had resigned myself to the realization that we were done. It was our hardest time. But something wonderful happened in it. And, although I am not recommending it, our being apart meant that we stopped arguing long enough to hear God trying to help us. And believe it or not, it was actually your father who sought help first."

"Dad?" Terry was surprised by her mother's revelation.

"Yes."

"My dad? The man we had to fake forgetting something or a bathroom emergency to make him pull over just so you'd have time to pull up directions."

"Girl yes! Isn't that what I said?"

Terry was laughing at her mother. "I'm just checking. I want to make sure you were talking about my daddy."

"He was not that bad." Morgan couldn't help but join in, "Ok, yeah. He was. He was pretty funny at times. And I do miss our family trips. One trip, and we had stories for the whole year."

"I know, right!" Terry lightheartedly agreed.

"Ahh. How I miss him," Morgan sighed. "Honey, when we got the details right, our marriage became amazing. We had the makings of something great from the start. It just got lost in those few things that made such a huge impact over time that kept us from moving forward freely together. Kind of like a beautiful butterfly fluttering its wings but only able to float to the next blade of grass. And you wonder why? Why this incredible creature is just sitting there. But if you pick it up and look closely, you see there's a hurt. And that hurt is keeping it from being and doing what it was created to be and do. Even after it matured and transformed, that hurt is keeping it from having the life it should have until the hurt heals." [1]

"What a beautiful illustration. I see what you mean." Terry said thoughtfully.

"Do you really? Look Baby. Listen to me. All through your incredible life, you have been and will be exposed to so many things that have the potential to knock the wind right out of you. And you've done amazingly well considering some of the things that I've seen you go through. But you have to be careful not to let any one of those things hold you back from living your life to the extent that God intended."

"Mom, I have a good life. A great job and great friends. And God is really looking out for me. I've even seen what I would consider a miraculous difference in me. Especially this week. There's no way...," Terry paused think about her next words. She really didn't want her mother to worry. But she had to be honest. "I mean, I would have lost my mind if the events of this week had happened a few years ago. My spiritual life is maturing." Terry explained.

"I'm really glad to hear that. And it's good that you are growing honey. But still, I want you to ask yourself if there is anything still sitting in your heart that you need to let go of. If there is one thing I've learned

---

[1] Clark, Brianna [Brianna Clark]. (2016, Aug 8). "Happy Monday! This is for Someone" post.
https://m.facebook.com/story.php?story_fbid=10209666243843680&id=15569 80452

over the years, is that tragedy and uproarious circumstances are prime opportunities for promotion and growth. Even though at the time you are going through, good is the last thing you can see in the situation." Morgan was not satisfied that her daughter was seeing everything as clearly as she thought she was.

"Mom, I just told you I'm good. I'm standing strong. It wasn't easy, but I conquered this week." Terry tried to convince her mother that she really was okay.

"And so you have. But my heart just isn't settled yet. So I want you to keep this in mind. According to the Bible, Job had everything. A great life with his family, friends, wealth, and status. But he also harbored a challenge to his faith and confidence in what God had blessed him with. He had fear in his heart. And he lost everything until he dealt with his heart issue. Only then was he able to live the life God intended, with twice what he had before. But do you know what I wonder about every time I think about this part of scripture?"

"What's that?" Terry reluctantly played along.

"If Job was supposed to actually have all three portions. And he lost a whole third of his intended life because of this one thing hidden in his heart. How much of our lives are we just giving away because we don't want to release, or sometimes even admit a heart issue exists?" This question sat heavily in the air. Terry seriously had to consider her mother's wisdom. [2]

Both ladies sat quietly thinking. Morgan's mind was on whether her first born was truly hearing her.

---

[2] (Gal 3:11 - the just shall live by faith, Romans 3:28 - a man is justified by faith
Job 3:25 - The thing that he feared, Job 42:10 - God turned the captivity of Job and gave him twice what he had)

But Terry was wondering why her mother kept pressing the issue even though she had already acknowledged that she heard her mother's words. She had found a certain peace in spite of the happenings around her. So she believed that things were under control. And even if there was more, she could handle it.

"Mom. I'm hearing you. Really. I get what you are saying. I'll be fine."

"I pray so. Because the next time I see you, I expect to see the light in my baby's eyes shining brightly." Morgan tried to lighten the mood.

"Don't worry mom. Everything will be just fine." Terry predicted with a smile.

"And speaking of seeing you, you still haven't told me when you are coming to visit us."

"Well, I was trying to schedule a break right after school starts next month. You know, after my labor day run. This year my workload has had a totally different flow. With all the changes happening at work, I've had to oversee more of our retail division this year. I usually can get away in July, but this year I have to wait until September. We've already started getting our regular holiday campaign plans together, so I can take a break and won't be so pressed when the calls come in this season."

"Good. You know you missed a great cruise with your cousins." Morgan had to remind her.

"I know. I saw the pictures. I hate missing the shenanigans with those guys. I'm definitely going to make it next time."

"Good. Because it wasn't the same without you."

"I know. And give Lavelle a hug and kiss for me. Even though that rascal didn't even call me after she got the present I sent her," Terry complained lightheartedly.

"I told her to call. I'll make sure she does. Alright honey. I'll talk with you later. Be safe and keep me updated. I love you." Morgan loved on her big baby from afar.

"I will. I love you too. Bye." Terry hung up and settled herself on her bed to get started on her work.

CHAPTER TWENTY TWO

Feeling a little more relaxed after talking to her mother, Terry opened her laptop to look over Dr. Ryan's product information. But before she could access the correct file for her to review, the program on the TV caught her attention. One of her favorite Pastors was on.

The program was halfway over but she wanted to see the rest of what Pastor Warren had to say.

"It's the subconscious mind at work. Now, if you don't watch out, you'll be driving down the interstate, fixing your eye makeup, and talking on the cell phone all at the same time."

"Me? I'm driving with my knee and putting my neck tie on because driving is now a subconscious action. That's why people have accidents. Because they can't drive subconsciously. That only works when there is nobody on the interstate but you." The congregation laughed.

"The point I'm trying to make is this. If I continue to teach the Word of God to you so that you are consciously listening and obeying, if I continue to do that, you will begin to produce scripturally subconsciously. The Apostle Paul said it like this. It is the Word of God that is working effectually in me. The word Energeo in the greek means that if I keep hearing it, the Word, the self-fulfilling power of God's word makes me behave myself. It makes me love when I don't want to love. Forgive when I don't want to forgive. And stand up when I don't think that I can. It is the power of the Word of God. All you have to do is just read it and believe it. The doing is up to God. So the problem is getting enough of the Word in you until your behavior becomes subconscious."

"The conscious and the subconscious mind.   I haven't

forgotten about The Blessing, but I need to lay a little foundation before I take you there."

"So now, things happen to me. I have human responses. I'm not superman all of the time." Pastor Warren laughed along with the congregation. "I do have human responses. Every now and then I encounter a piece of kryptonite just like everybody else does. But after I have my human moment, subconsciously, the Word of God lifts up a standard. And though something may not be working, it may have troubled me for a day. But after a day, something in the Word rises up in my spirit. And I begin to say about myself what the Word says about me. And when things aren't working, I get something up in my spirit that says my soul why art thou disquieted? Wait thou upon God. For my expectation is from above." There were sounds of agreement around the sanctuary.

"That's why you can't handle trials and tests. Because you don't have enough in you. And you freak out when things don't work. Because you're not anchored in the truth. I drill the Word into myself. I force my mind to house it. I force my spirit to be full of scripture. When I want to stop, and my mind wants to stop reading, my heart says you need more scripture or you won't make it through this test. Most of the tests guys, most of the tests are permitted by God to get you to a place of preparation for something."

Terry sat up straighter.

"So you can't see it as God not loving you or just letting random stuff to happen to you. You have to see it as preparation for something big. So, don't ask for less challenges. Ask for more anointing. Don't ask for less tests. Ask for more power. Don't ask for less in inconvenient situations. Ask for more wisdom. You don't want to go down in your ability. So start fighting the one that's the champ.

Don't keep fighting the ones that you can whip. You need to fight the one who keeps sneaking a left and you don't know how he keeps hitting you. And when you look at the video you see after you swing your right hook, you drop your left. Now you go, ohh. Now I'm ready for this fool the next time. Because he thinks he's gonna sucker punch me with that right hook because I always drop my left. But this time, consciously, I'm gonna drop it to get him to come in with the right because he thinks I'm doing what I always do. But what I'm doing this time is using the fact that I know what I was doing wrong because God allowed me to go through that situation. And what the devil thinks he's going to use this time to knock me out, is now a deception by me to knock him out. Push three people and tell them to get some more of the Word." The congregation turned to encourage one another.

"The Bible says the Word of God is the sword that Holy Spirit wields. Good God almighty! Stomp your foot and say I'm coming out of this thing tonight. Declare this yolk is destroyed tonight. This burden is being lifted off of my shoulders right here tonight."[3]

The congregation began to declare those things as the broadcast faded to the commercial. Terry found herself declaring along with them.

She picked up the remote and hit the off button. She sat quietly amazed about how God was making sure she got his message. Again, special ordered. Because that was right on time. First her mother and now this broadcast. And, boy, did she need to hear that. "So. That was definitely for me." She confessed to the empty room. Pushing her laptop aside, she got up from her bed. Sitting down at her vanity, in her mind she methodically went through the events of

---

[3] Excerpt from "The Blessing is on Your Life", 6-15-2016, Apostle K. L. Warren, KLWarrenMinistries.org

the past week. Then facing herself in the mirror, she sighed heavily and began detailing her evaluation of those events to her reflection.

"You definitely have had several human moments this week. Especially Saturday." She sat there for a moment, laughingly shaking her head at her reflection. "So, I guess now is as good a time as any for your "let a man examine himself" moment." She looked herself in the eyes. "So. Here we go. Let's talk this thing out. The most obvious thing that comes to mind is fear. You've accepted a certain amount of fear when you go to the doctor. But everything goes great everytime you go. So, why?" She paused to think for a moment. And remembering her earlier conversation with Anthony she continued.

"First things first. Get over your past. What happened before is not happening now. Your present life is so good. And you are so much wiser. You're not a helpless child anymore. So you don't have to be afraid. On top of that, you can't keep living in fear and still expect your faith to work effectively in your life. You possess the power of the spirit of Christ. So you have to choose. Lesser authority must yield to greater authority. And God in you is greater than anything that comes at you. Which means when fear comes, it cannot stay unless you give it permission to do so."

Even though she wasn't speaking loudly, it felt like her voice echoed in the quiet room. Right then she felt a little silly for sitting there talking to herself. But silly for a moment was worth victory for her lifetime. So she took a deep breath and continued.

"I decree that fear no longer has power over me. I will not be afraid of going to any doctor. God said that I am to prosper and be in good health even as my soul prospers. So be it. I have nothing to fear. God loved me enough to decree that with the stripes of Christ I am already healed. There is a purpose for my life that I have to fulfill. I am protected. And no matter what I see, I know that I have the power and victory by God's word. Fear no longer has any power over me."

Just being able to say those words was empowering for her. So this is what on purpose renewing of your faith feels like. She let out a huge sigh of release. "Wow. Now that was a weight lifted. So, now. Moving on. Let us continue." She told her reflection.

She paused to think about the car accident. "What was the lesson in that?" Nothing came to her right away. She couldn't think of anything she should have done better. No major freak out. After all, who wouldn't react to a car headed their way. She did call out Jesus instead of cursing. She laughed at that thought.

Forgiveness.

"Hmmm? It can't be that." She actually felt sorry for Jarod. "Maybe this was about being a help to them. I'm not hurt and my car will be fine. And Patrice has turned out to be a positive presence in my life. So God, we're good on this one." She was satisfied or at least content with her analysis.

She rose from her seat to move around her room while she continued.

"Now, this work thing. Cameron Robertson is truly a thorn in my flesh. But I do know this. Integrity will prevail. It always does. And regardless of this deal, my business affairs will not suffer." These words she had no problem speaking confidently. No matter the challenge, she always found a way to come out on the path to success in business. Whether it took a few days or a few months.

You know there's more.

Terry stopped pacing and stood silently for a minute. This time, the words were obviously more than just a contemplation of her heart. But her response was determined if not totally sure.

"Where is this coming from? Everything at work is under control." She said those words slowly and softly. But her heart would not let that pass and her pulse quickened. The worse kind of deception is

self deception. She closed her eyes, trying to calm her heart beat.
But only the complete truth would do that. She wasn't ready for that.

"Come on now!" She stomped her foot and walked back over to plop
down on the foot of her bed. "Why do we have to talk about him? I've
got everything under control. He won't be... No. He is not a problem.
Strictly business is all there is."

Forgive him already.

"But.."

Jarod was for you.

She caught her breath momentarily. The image of Jarod sitting on the
ground with his head in his hands sobbing made Terry's eyes fill with
tears. Then she remembered Patrice saying how she prayed for him
to move on. And how relieved she was that he finally could.

"He must feel so free right now." Terry mused softly.

You can too. Let go.

"I did. I mean..." Terry dropped her head into her hands. And her
words came out just above a whisper. "I moved on. I healed. I dated.
I didn't mistreat anyone else because of him. I tried to be fair and
open. I've been happy. I wasn't walking around angry or in pain and
making everyone else suffer. I made up in my mind a long time ago
that I wasn't going to be that person. So I let it go. I let it ... go."

Tears were now slowly sliding down her cheeks. The words she had
spoken were true. But not complete. And the more she spoke, the
more she realized that her heart had more to release. Finally
surrendering and accepting her truth, she felt this hold suddenly
brake. She felt both laughter and tears rising from deep inside of her.
So she let the tears flow as hard and loud as they wanted to. For the

first time this week, her tears weren't ones of frustration. It felt so good to just let them go.

By the time her tears stopped, she had slid down until she was sitting on the floor at the foot of the bed. Relaxing her head against her soft comforter, she quietly enjoyed this new feeling. The feeling of a cleansing cry coupled with having that heavy weight lifted from her heart was so calming. When she opened her eyes, there was a soft smile on her face.

"I forgive you. Michael. Whew." She took a deep breath before she released her next words into the air. "And the sooner I do this, the better. Even though your mess was just evil, it is definitely a lot harder to do this one. But, you too. Reginald. So now Lord, I'm going to need you to keep that one out of my path for a long while so I can make sure it sticks." As serious as she was about her request, she couldn't hold back the sudden fit of laughter that escaped her at the picture that popped into her head.

"Lord, you know my heart's intent. But you also know your child. And if I see Reggie too soon, I'm going to be in danger of a relapse to my former taser carrying, shock 'em first and give him a piece of my mind while he's shaking on the floor anointing. Ha ha, ahem." Clearing her throat, she had to catch herself from enjoying the visual she painted too much. "You know what I need. And, um, I, uh… I just thank you," she sobered. "Thank you for showing me what I was holding on to. And for getting me through this. All of it."

She stood up, brushed herself off and turned back towards the mirror. She no longer felt so self conscious about talking to her reflection.

"So. Now we get back to work and to life. But without the blinders on. Ahh," she sighed, "God you are so good. And I cannot wait to see what happens next. But whatever it is, I know it's going to knock Anthony's socks off. It has to be that big. Big trials, big victories. I believe that." Smiling at her reflection one last time, she turned to go back to her work.

This time when she opened her laptop, she almost felt giddy with expectation. No, she did not expect life to be perfect. But she had been reminded that she always had help because God was mindful of her. And that those weren't merely words on the page of the Bible. Today was the help and the proof that she needed.

She spent the next 90 minutes going over the contents of Dr. Ryan's folder and plotting out her initial plan. She looked over her notes before putting things away. Pleased with her ideas, she sent an email to Anthony and then closed her computer. It was still a little early for her, but she was tired. And 9 o'clock was a great time for her to shut it down for the night.

"Tomorrow is looking good. It will be a great day. That is my confession." She put her briefcase away and grabbed a bottle of water from the supply she kept in her workout room. Once she settled down under her comforter, she turned off her light and started her last prayer for the night. She was more ready to sleep than she thought. Her eyes weren't closed more than thirty seconds before she drifted off to a peaceful sleep.

CHAPTER TWENTY THREE
NEXT THURSDAY

The sound of rain lightly tapping her window pulled Terry from her sleep. Her alarm had yet to go off. She felt so good right now and didn't want to open her eyes yet. Feeling like she wanted to drift back into a pleasant dream, she slowly shifted lower under the covers and buried her face deeper into her pillow. But it wasn't working so she just spent the time praying, thinking about the possibilities of the day ahead and enjoying the relaxing sound of the new morning until she was ready to rise to face the day.

Her alarm caught her in the shower. She couldn't wait for it to go off and jumped out of bed early ready to go. She was both relaxed and excited. Anticipation was coursing through her veins. It was still early so she decided to get in a quick run on the treadmill. She stepped out of the tub and wrapped herself in her plush towel. "Man. Everything just feels better. I can't wait to see what you have in store for me today Father!"

Terry finished getting dressed and made her way downstairs. Making herself a smoothie, she sang and laughed along with the crew of her favorite morning radio show. Those guys were hilarious. Nephew has absolutely no filter.

Everything felt normal again. No. Better than normal. For the moment.

Her phone rang and she checked her watch. The display said 7:16. Immediately her guard went up. What could not wait for forty-five minutes? She grabbed her phone and saw that it was Kayla. "Lord?" she whispered as she answered with a cautious smile.

"Hello?"

"Good morning Terry." Kayla greeted her cheerfully allowing Terry to breathe again. She didn't realized that she was holding her breath.

"Good morning Kayla. What's going on?" She needed Kayla to get straight to the punchline.

"Nothing to worry about. I wanted to make sure you were planning on getting in at your normal time. I checked the voicemail this morning and there was a message about a special delivery being made first thing this morning. I knew you would want to know about it."

"Absolutely. Thank you ma'am."

"My pleasure. See you in a few." Kayla hung up.

Terry grabbed her smoothie and took a big gulp that was way too much. She quickly leaned over the sink, fighting back her coughs until she could swallow all of the liquid. Coughing to get her breathing together she mused, "Well it looks like the moment of truth is here. Better let Anthony know." She sent Anthony a short text and finished cleaning up the few dishes she had used.

All ready and mentally prepared for the day ahead, she gave herself a final once over before heading back downstairs. Making sure everything was off, she grabbed her briefcase and keys off the kitchen table, hit the garage door button and headed down to her car. The rain had stopped but the heavy moisture of the mid-August Georgia air quickly invaded the small space. She jumped quickly into her car before the humidity could attack her curls. Checking her time, she nodded with satisfaction. "7:31. Right on target. Let's get this day going."

Fifteen minutes later, she pulled into her parking spot and quickly exited her car. The elevator was already open so she walked on, pushed her floor and checked her reflection as the doors closed. But at the last second, a man in a black suit and tie stopped the doors with his case and stepped on. He nodded and without a word turned forward and stood waiting for the elevator to move.

Terry did not recognize the man and was curious about his identity. Especially since it appeared he was going to her floor. As a rule of thumb, Clients rarely had meetings scheduled in their offices before 8:45 am. It wasn't even 8am yet. Self preservation kicked in and she repositioned her keys in her hand. Just in case.

The elevator doors opened on her floor and the man stepped out. Terry slowly followed and her heart began to beat faster as she realized he was headed toward her office. This must be a courier, she thought. She became calm because she knew her safety wasn't in question but at the same time more anxious because of what was possibly in the case the man carried.

But that was nothing compared to the brick that dropped in her stomach when she turned the last corner before her office. To her total surprise, sitting in her reception area was the last person she would have thought she'd have even the slightest chance of seeing that day.

Caramel brown, six foot two, and built like a Cam Newton. Good Lord, his pictures did not do this man justice. Evan Blake had his watchful eye on the courier who had dropped his case on the desk and pulled out an envelope. Unfolding his full frame, he rose from his seat when he noticed Terry. But the courier stepped to her first.

"Good morning. I have a confidential letter for Ms. Terry Ellis."

"Good morning. I am Terry Ellis." She turned to acknowledge the mountain standing nearby. "And good morning. I will be right with you." She turned back to sign for the envelope.

"Ma'am, I will need to see your identification." The courier politely informed her. That was unusual, she thought. She showed him her license, signed her name and took the envelope, sliding it into her bag for the moment.

As soon as the courier left, she turned her full attention to Evan. Approaching him with her hand extended.

Hiding her nervousness, she greeted him with her brightest professional smile. "Good morning Mr. Blake. It is a pleasure to meet you. How are you?"

"Good morning. I'm a little tired, but well. How are you this morning?" His voice was as commanding as his stature.

"I am wonderful. Please, come in and have a seat." As she stepped into her office behind Evan, Kayla rounded the corner and her eyebrows shot up to the ceiling. Terry gave Kayla a slight shrug and carried on with Evan.

"Please, have a seat. Can I get you anything?" Terry asked, sliding her belongings under her desk.

"I would say coffee, but I plan to rest after my next meeting. Do you have water?"

"Yes I do." She reached into her mini-fridge and brought a cold bottle to him. Her mind was spinning with wonder about why this man whose business has been priority one on her list the last couple of days was suddenly sitting in her office. Uninvited. Taking her seat again, she set out to get to the reason he was there.

"Is there anything else I can get for you Mr. Blake?"

"No. I'm fine. And please, call me Evan."

"Alright Evan. It is truly a pleasure to finally meet you."

"Thank you."

"So tell me, how can I assist you today?"

"I had another meeting come up today and I decided to come straight here from the airport in hopes that you could see me earlier than scheduled." Evan explained. But Terry was clueless and her heart began to race in a slight panic. Keeping her composure, she picked up the schedule that was lying face down on her desk and looked it over.

"I'm sorry. Please forgive me. But I was not aware that you were coming in today. We rarely have this kind of mixup with our schedule. But you are here now so tell me what you need, I am certain I can assist you." Terry's voice was much steadier than her heart was at that moment. She definitely could not afford to mess up her first impression with Evan.

"I don't understand. When I spoke with Ryan yesterday, he told me you were okay with 11:30. But I was hoping to get this taken care of earlier so I could free up my afternoon." The irritation in Evan's voice registered loud and clear. But so did the name he spoke.

'Wait a minute. Are you talking about Dr. Ryan McGhee?" Terry asked glancing down at the schedule.

"Yes," was his curt response.

"Now I understand. When he was here yesterday, he referred to his partner but he never actually spoke your name. Mystery solved." Terry smiled and reached for her briefcase to pull out Dr. Ryan's folder and her notes.

"Excellent. Now, let me tell you what I had in mind." Evan's demeanor softened and he pulled some papers from his jacket pocket and slid them across her desk. "I've already discussed most of this with Ryan. He will still come by later this morning so I'll just give you what I have and let you work it in with what you and Ryan come up with.”

“Alright. Let’s take a look.” Terry took the pages and flipped through them. But something was off. She noticed that the rendering of the apparatus was of an earlier test model. Dr. Ryan had given her a nearly complete packet. And it would stand to reason that if Evan was in fact the partner the doctor spoke of, he would have had all of the current information. Terry looked up at Evan, smiled and then went back to the pages. She then took her notepad and held it next to the pages Evan had handed her. Nodding slowly, she smiled softly and focused her attention back to her guest. This time when she sat down her notes, she put them face down and sat Evan’s pages on top of them before she spoke.

“Evan, like I told Dr. Ryan yesterday, this product is very unique and I believe it will make a huge impact on the medical community. We could do wonders with the campaign. My partner Anthony will be here for the meeting at 11:30 so that we can put together a game plan and move forward. Several of your notes are right along the lines of a few of mine and have given me some additional ideas to discuss later on.”

“Well it’s good to know that we are somewhat on the same page. Are there any points you want to talk over before I go?” Evan asked matter of factly.

“Actually,” she slid his pages toward him, “I’d rather ask if there are any that you would especially want me to focus on? It’s much better for me to hear what’s on your mind first. That way I get to hear strictly what you want without any bias.”

Evan looked down at his papers and smiled. “No. I think my thoughts are pretty self explanatory. I’ll give Ryan a call and let him know we’ve spoken. I’m looking forward to working with you.” He rose and extended his hand.

Terry stood and shook Evan's hand. "Likewise. I look forward to you having more time so that all of us will get to be in the same room making the magic happen together."

"Yeah. I like you." Evan said, nodding thoughtfully and firmly shaking her hand. "I think this will work out just fine. So I'll just have to make sure that happens."

"Wonderful. Looks like we are in business." Terry released his hand and grabbed the papers sitting on the desk and stacked them neatly back on top of Dr. Ryan's folder. Although she had to make an inquiry to be sure of his connection to this project, she was definitely glad that Evan had shown up in her office. She also wasn't about to let him just walk away without a way to contact him. "Until our next meeting."

"Until then. You have a good day Terry." Evan turned to exit.

"Thank you. Oh, Evan. Do you have a card you could leave with me?" Terry asked as matter of factly as possible.

Evan stopped his exit and turned back with a smile to respond to her request. "Actually, Terry, I did not bring my cards with me. But if you need to contact me, Ryan has my number. Just have him give me a call. We'll talk soon." He nodded and continued his exit.

Terry took her seat, thinking about the last fifteen minutes. Is this really the Evan Blake project that she and Anthony have been chasing? Maybe. She hoped so. It's a great project to be attach to. And how incredible was this to have him come to them. But she still had to be sure before sharing any information with him. He seemed a bit odd. But geniuses often were. She just had to wait until eleven thirty to find out for sure.

CHAPTER TWENTY FOUR

At about a quarter to nine, Anthony walked into her office.

"Well, hello to you Mr. Sunshine. Glad you could finally join us." Terry playfully scolded him.

Not letting her get the best of him, he shot back as he dropped into the chair in front of her. "I'm sorry. I know you can't wait to see me everyday. I have that effect on people." He gave her his special smile.

"Oh come on, man. It is too early for the Broder show. Besides, I thought you would be rushing in to get our special delivery." She tapped the envelope sitting next to her phone.

"So, what was it?" Anthony asked pretending he wasn't pressed to know.

"I don't know. I haven't opened it yet. I've been waiting patiently since the man in the black suit dropped it off for you to get here. Selfish." She shook her head at him.

"What? Who me? Not at all. I am here for you." He put his hand over his heart and leaned forward in mock innocence.

"Boy quit playing and just open the envelope." She slid the envelope towards him. She wanted to know what was inside just as much as she was apprehensive about its contents.

He took it and turned it over to see who it was from. Taking his time was putting Terry on edge. She stood up and leaned over her desk.

"Man if you don't open that envelope!"

"Alright! Alright!" He tore open the seal and slid the contents out. And then he just sat. He sat there staring for a long time before he slowly lifted the top page to look at pages in the middle and then at the end of the documents. The longer he remained silent, the harder Terry's heart beat. She couldn't take it anymore and was about to snatch the papers out of his hand and read them for herself when he looked up and sat the papers on the desk.

"What?"

Anthony didn't respond. He just sat there shaking his head.

"What Anthony?!"

He just pushed the papers toward her, "You are not going to believe this."

She snatched up the papers and began reading. And he was right. She could not believe her eyes. "Did you see this?"

"Uh, yeah. I'm the one who told you that you wouldn't believe your eyes." Anthony responded sarcastically.

Terry was speechless. She looked back down at the contract in her hands and then back up at Anthony several times while reading. Finally sitting the papers down, she turned to grab a bottle of water because her mouth suddenly felt dry.

Not only did they get the Tadashi deal that they worked so hard on, the contract also had an addendum to hire them to work on the second largest resort joint venture in Korea under the Tadashi parent company. All she had to do was sign.

Terry felt like she just stepped off of a small playground merry go round spinning at high speed. Laying her head in her hand, she had to ask again.

"Ant, is this real?"

He turned to the signature page. "It's real alright. That's his seal."

When Terry lifted her head she wore a huge smile. "Now, you can't tell me that God is not good. Ah!" She excitedly laid back in her seat and shook her feet in the air. Then she shook the contract at him while her eyes suddenly lit up like christmas trees. "And on top of this, you will not believe who was waiting for me when I walked in this morning. Go ahead. Guess!" There was so much excitement flowing through her at that moment she couldn't figure out what to do with her hands. She could have floated to the ceiling. To say that she was having a great morning was an understatement.

Anthony was looking at her like she had lost her mind. He'd seen her happy before but this was on another level. What the heck had her smiling like that. Yes, getting this contract was exciting but this was too much. Who had her acting like that? He found himself getting a little irritated by the thought. They've been through enough this week. And there was no room for more drama or let downs. And that jubilance wasn't caused by a woman's visit. Of that he was sure. He was going to get to the bottom of this mystery, and quickly. He thought to himself, "I guess the good doctor didn't fully get my message yesterday. I'll just have to fix that."

"Who Terry? Who could possibly make you this... giddy?" Anthony asked suspiciously.

"Come on Ant. Take one guess. Just one. You won't believe it!" Despite his attitude, Terry couldn't quash her excitement.

"You're right. I can't believe anyone has you acting like a kid in a candy store. Like the president walked in here or something. This contract is great news but you are too...whatever right now. We've been friends, practically family, for nearly five years and I've never seen you like this. And now you want me to just join in on your joy parade. I'm not playing this game. Just tell me. You would think.."

"Evan Blake!" She interrupted him.

"Wait..what?" He sat up on the edge of his seat. Terry was nodding her head to confirm that he heard her right. "Why didn't you call me? I would have been here before now if you had said something. You could have sent a text and I would have been here before he left." He scolded.

"Uh, I did text you this morning." She corrected.

"That was about a delivery!"

"Which you knew was important! So look, don't be mad at me because you took the scenic route to work this morning." The smile never left her face.

"Really Terry? It's like that?" His attempt to take the focus off himself didn't work.

"Yes! Really! I told you there was an important delivery coming and you took your sweet precious time getting here. So don't you give me the third degree. I showed up, regardless of what was waiting for us." Terry's demeanor sobered, but only slightly.

"I know Terry! I know." He acknowledged. "I just couldn't take seeing you disappointed again. I figured that by now you would have already found out what the outcome was. We had some warning so I knew you wouldn't be devastated or anything like that if the news wasn't good. Man!" He jumped up and walked over to the window. Terry was feeling better but it was obvious that he couldn't seem to let go of the tension that had built up over the last week. "Look, I know I talk a good game but, when it comes to you and my mom, sometimes it gets just a little difficult to keep cool. I'm just glad we got the Tadashi deal. We worked really hard on it."

"Yes we did. And thank you for caring so much."

"Yeah. But if you tell anybody what I just said, you will regret it," he warned.

"Yeah, yeah. I hear you." She brushed off his threat. "And now after all of our searching, we have Evan Blake himself showing up in our office."

"So what did he want? He didn't just appear out of thin air for nothing." Anthony asked, bracing himself with his arms folded across his chest and his back against the window.

"Actually, now it's you who won't believe this. The elusive Evan Blake project we've been chasing down turned out to be sitting right under our noses." She looked down and tapped the folder sitting in front of her.

"You're kidding me." Anthony shot up straight. "You mean we already have Blake's project?"

"Dude, that's what I'm saying."

"That's incredible Terry!" Anthony's face lit up.

"I know. I know. I do have one concern though. But we can take care of that when Dr. Ryan gets here at 11:30."

"So what's wrong?" Anthony took his seat to brace himself. He knew it was too good to be true.

"It's not really wrong, but the rendering of the apparatus he had his notes on was several generations old. I just need to do my due diligence. Everything falls into place for me except that. And it's a simple fix to verify Dr. Ryan's partner before I start running off at the mouth about our work. I'm sure when people hear Evan's name, nine times out of ten, they do whatever it takes to keep him happy. He just has that kind of power. But he's not the last available client in the world. And our reputations mean everything to me."

"So. What do you have to show the good doctor?" Anthony asked reaching for the notes in his briefcase.

"Here. Take a look at this." She handed him the folder with all the notes she made last night.

"Wow! Damn we're good. Sometimes it's scary how much we think alike but still have such distinct differences that compliment each other. Like we planned it or something." He gave her all the notes he brought in with a huge smile on his face. When she looked at what he had put on paper, she just laughed.

"This is so cool. Man, this is going to be amazing. I cannot wait until Dr. Ryan gets here." Terry declared, trying to contain her excitement. Discussing Evan wasn't the only thing she was looking forward to when she saw him next. Her face showed it. And Anthony saw it.

"Hey! What's that all about?"

"Huh? What? What are you talking about now?" Terry tried to hide her smile.

"Not this dude too? I'll tell you what, I'm calling Momma V on your behind. And, since I haven't heard that you've talked to your mother, I think we need to check in with her too." Anthony threatened.

"Ha! Too late! I already called her last night. Boom!" Terry laughingly responded.

"Oh Yeah? I bet you didn't tell her about the good doctor giving you butterflies and things unholy. I think maybe she needs to know." Anthony threatened again, this time reaching for his phone with a devious grin.

"You dial one number and I'll make you pay for the next month. No 'Lunch' for you buddy. And if you think I can't do it, remember the Johnson-Edison account last year?" Terry sat back in her chair and folded her arms. And Anthony's face dropped when he realized what she was insinuating.

"You did that on purpose?" Anthony was looking at the architect of his dry spell last year. He canceled more dates that month than he had the whole year before and after it.

"I'm just saying that we needed the best mind on deck. It was well worth it. Wasn't it?" Her innocence was so suspect. And he could see the laughter in her eyes as she continued. "The bonus you received set a new precedent here, and set you apart from the rest of your colleagues."

Shaking his head in amazement, Anthony softly responded with wonder. "I had no idea of your true power when I sat there yesterday applauding your subtle prowess. Even me, your talented friend and brother, have fallen victim. I'm rubbing off on you way too much."

"Let's just say that I've learned to use my powers for good." She winked.

"Amazing." Anthony said, slowly shaking his head. "What on earth have I done?"

"Believe it or not, you've just left the twilight zone." She said barely keeping a straight face.

"Huh? What? That doesn't make a bit of sense!" Anthony protested. And a huge smile broke out on Terry's face. Her joy meter was on one hundred.

"I know, right. But I'm just so happy right now that I don't even care! Ha! Anthony! This is probably the one and only time you will ever see me lose it like this. But man! God is so awesome! I want to close my

door and just jump up and down right now. I could Holla if it wouldn't
have people running in here to see what's going on. I just, I just…"
She had to wipe at her eyes because they began to tear up. "Man, I
just can't tell you how good I feel right now. But I can tell you this. All
the challenging things from the last week have worked out for my
good. It was not easy, but I got rid of a snake, landed awesome new
business, met incredible new people, and most of all… Anthony, most
importantly, I broke free of the emotional prison that I didn't even
realize I was still locked in. Do you know how long I fooled myself into
thinking I was ok? Whew!" She released a jubilant sigh.

"I'm glad Terry. It's really awkward seeing you like this, but I think I
like it. I can tell that a huge weight has been lifted off your shoulders.
And I'm really happy you can smile like this. It's strange, but in a good
way."

"Yeah. I don't think I've ever felt like this before. And I cannot wait to
see what happens next. I have so much expectation right now. I am
ready for anything."

"And I'm here with you no matter what." He said soberly. "I'll be able
to sleep well tonight. Uh, once you sign that contract that is. How
about this? Let's just get this out of the way right now."

Anthony's demeanor perked up as he reached for the contract from
the desk and flipped to the last page and pushed it in front of her.

"Dude, don't you think we need to read this again once the shock has
worn off." Terry asked with laughter in her eyes.

"OK, yeah. Hurry up and shake it off. Let's get to reading and put this
baby under lock and key. I cannot afford any more gray hairs."

"Alright. I'll get started and hand over the first few pages so you can
also have time to start reading it through before our appointment. I
want Chad to look at this asap. We're signing this today. Have him

come to your office in thirty minutes. I'm not letting this contract out of our sight."

"Works for me." Anthony rose from his seat, grabbed his briefcase and headed towards the door. "I'll be back in a few. I need coffee. My head is starting to spin. Just when I thought it was over, two more men walk into your life and cause a ruckus. I'm not complaining though. I just need more caffeine to keep up with you."

"Hey." Terry stopped his exit. "I told you. God is good. Only God could make a symphony out of the mess we've been dealing with."

Anthony gave her a half smile. "Yeah. I know. You're right." He winked, turned and left.

"Yes." Terry whispered in victory. "Another one for the home team Father."

Terry grabbed the contract and a notepad and commenced her review. By ten o'clock, she had finished and given the papers to Anthony along with her notes to discuss with Chad. She also called Karen, Tadashi's assistant to acknowledge receipt of the contract. After she conveyed her appreciation for being chosen and hung up, Terry sat perplexed. She sensed a new level of respect in her voice when Karen offered up, "Please do not hesitate to contact us for anything you may need from us." Weren't we the ones being hired. That was supposed to be her line. Boy this day just keeps getting weirder.

CHAPTER TWENTY FIVE

Just before eleven thirty, Kayla walked in to let her know that Dr. Ryan had arrived.

"Good morning Dr. Ryan. How are you?" Terry greeted him as he walked in. He took her outstretched hand and held it firmly.

"I'm great Terry. I couldn't wait to get here and get started with you."

Her heart fluttered for a moment. Work with me. Working with me is what he is saying. Reminding herself to keep her wits, she noticed the look on his face when he realized what he said. "Dr. Ryan, it is going to be a pleasure working with you on this project. Please have a seat so we can get started. Anthony will be joining us momentarily."

"Great. I also talked with my partner last night. And he is on board with everything."

"Dr. Ryan. May I ask you if your partner is a "Silent Partner"?"

"No, not at all. Why do you ask?"

"Well, you refer to him as your partner but you have yet to mention his name."

"Ah. I'm sorry. No, he is not a silent partner. His name is Evan Blake. I'm sure you are familiar with the name." Terry allowed herself to smile but sat very still so she wouldn't risk losing her composure. She was in a strange place today and had to make sure she didn't go overboard.

"Yes I am. In fact, Evan came here this morning."

"What? When I talked to him last night he said he wasn't able to make the appointment today." Dr. Ryan explained.

"Well, to my surprise, he was waiting when I arrived this morning. He decided to come directly from the airport so that he could drop off his notes in person. And now that you have confirmed that he is in fact your business partner, I can freely speak with him about our work."

"So, you didn't talk with him?" Dr. Ryan asked with a little concern.

"Oh yes, we spoke. But only in general terms." She tried to reassure him. "Dr. Ryan, we have a confidentiality agreement that I will not violate. Evan is a powerful man, but you hired us without specifically giving him access to your account information. He did leave some notes with me but they were written on an earlier version of the apparatus rendering. And I just couldn't in good conscience discuss your work without talking with you first and verifying his identity."

"I understand. It's good to know you stand by your word. And I'm glad we've cleared this up. We definitely cannot have him left out of the process. So, now that we've clarified that, let's get to work." Dr. Ryan sat forward in his chair, rubbing his hands together in anticipation. At that moment Anthony walked into the room.

"Ah! Here comes my partner in crime and success. Dr. Ryan McGhee, meet Anthony Broder." Terry introduced her colleague.

"It's a pleasure to meet you Dr. Ryan." Anthony warmly greeted him and firmly shook his hand while giving him the once over. His internal alarm began to ring. So this is the talented doctor who's putting a smile on Terry's face. Yep. Gotta watch this one.

"Likewise Anthony. I've heard such great things about your work together. I can't wait to see you two in action." The smile on Dr. Ryan's face was almost too much for Terry to handle. He was playing it cool but you could feel the excitement radiating from him.

Anthony caught Terry's stare just before she looked away. He made a mental note, "Oh yeah, I'm keeping my eye on this dude."

"So, let's get started." Terry motioned to Dr. Ryan to take a seat and everyone settled in for their meeting.

Once they began, everything seemed to move like the script was already written for the day. Their ideas flowed effortlessly. After a while, Kayla stepped in to ask if Terry wanted her to order something for lunch since it was so late.

"What?" Terry checked her watch. Noticing the time, her hunger registered. "Wow! I didn't realize how late it was. I'm definitely hungry. Kayla, give us a minute and I'll let you know."

"Dr. Ryan, we didn't know how long you were available today so we did not plan ahead for lunch. We could have something brought in fairly quickly or step out to one of our local favorites. That is, unless you've run out of time for today." Anthony dutifully offered with a smile, making sure he also included a reason to decline. After all, he was under no obligation to spend additional time with Terry.

"Oh, No. I wanted to make sure you had whatever you needed from me so I left my afternoon open in case our meeting ran long. Either option is fine with me." Dr. Ryan happily responded.

"Great!" Terry jumped in. "I know the perfect spot. It's just around the corner. The service is good, fast, and the food is wonderful. Anthony, ask Kayla to give them a call. I want to be seated as soon as we get there, if possible. It should be by this time of day. But it doesn't hurt to be sure."

"Sure boss." Anthony answered with a hint of sarcasm.

That made Terry look at him with questioning eyes. "Now what?" she wondered. "Oh well. I'll deal with that after Dr. Ryan leaves. And after I eat," she smiled to herself and set about securing their working notes and her computer.

CHAPTER TWENTY SIX

They made it to the restaurant in just a few minutes and were seated right away. Terry and Anthony frequented the place and had a great relationship with the owner and GM. It's a wonder what passing on a few helpful gratis tips does for your business relationships.

The conversation was lively and informative. You can learn a great deal about a person over a good meal. Carefully guiding the conversation along, Terry listened intently for any signs of hidden crazy. It was a skill she acquired during her college internship and cultivated over the years. But she made sure to remind herself to stay focused on the big picture since the process was always more fragile when personal interest was sparked. And boy, could she smell smoke.

The strength of the doctor's character and compassion showed through more and more the longer he talked. And so did Anthony's sarcasm, drawing looks of confusion from Terry. She could not understand why he was being so hard on Dr. Ryan. And then it happened.

"Well, I have a meeting I have to get back to shortly. There was only one other thing I wanted to touch on." Anthony said, tenting his hands over his plate. This was not going to be good. Terry got an eerie feeling in her stomach and started to speak up. But Anthony dove in before she could.

"We are very protective of our reputation and work hard at keeping our business and personal relationships separated. It's the only way to maintain the integrity of both and be able to make the necessary decisions needed for success in both areas."

"Anthony! What are you doing?" Terry questioned jokingly. "Dr. Ryan, please excuse him. As you already know, I've been through a great deal recently and Anthony is quite protective of me as his business partner and close friend. He and Angela are quite the force to be reckoned with as you can see." She plastered on a smile that she hoped Dr. Ryan couldn't see through. She was embarrassed and a little upset that Anthony would mention personal intentions without discussing it with her first. But Dr. Ryan did not let her down.

"It's ok Terry. I understand completely. We're sitting here laughing like old friends and he just met me. In fact, considering our pending business connection at the time, you have to admit that the way we first met was very odd. Protecting those we care about is just what we, as men, do. And I can respect that Anthony. So Terry, don't worry about it." Dr. Ryan reassured her. And although Anthony didn't get a red flag, he still set his mind to keep his eyes open.

"Alright. So is everyone done?" Terry decided this was a good time to shift the scene. The guys said yes and she called the server over to close out their check. "Ok. Ready?" They all rose to leave and Anthony said his goodbye and walked out ahead of them. Terry and Dr. Ryan felt less pressured to hurry so they took their time walking back. And Dr. Ryan took this opportunity to find out just how committed Terry was to keeping their interactions strictly business.

"So Terry, Anthony brought up a good point. Have any of your clients ever become friends?" Dr. Ryan asked matter of factly. And Terry fought to hide her surprise at his question.

"Um, not really. I mean, friend is such an overused word these days. So let me answer like this. I've had occasions where other business has caused me to interact socially with clients. But in the eight years that I have been in this business, there has only been one. And you've already met her. I was doing some work for the city and Angela was my contact. We really got to know each other. And we've been inseparable ever since. And I wouldn't change a thing about that. It's been the most important crossing of the business and personal boundary lines in my life."

"So far." Dr. Ryan stopped and turned to face her. Terry's smile froze and then slowly faded as the impact of what her companion was insinuating hit her. But his smile grew. And now that the gate was open, he decided to dive through it. "I'm usually a pretty straight forward person. However, I'm not going to press the issue too much right now because we do have important business to handle. And I respect you professionally. But I do want you to know that, well, let me say it like this. While still respecting the gauntlet thrown down by Anthony, I want to say that I'm very interested in also exploring a personal relationship with you sometime in the near future." Terry was speechless. So she really wasn't the only one.

"Dr. Ryan," Terry began softly. Just then a co-worker walked by and said hello, drawing her attention away from the conversation momentarily. When she turned back to continue her response, he spoke first.

"Terry, listen. I know that we just met. It wasn't my intent to put you on the spot. And don't feel like you have to respond to what I said. I don't usually do this. I just wanted...," he paused, "felt like I needed to get that off my chest. Ok? There's no pressure. The focus will be on work." Dr. Ryan tried to put Terry at ease even though he was feeling even more self conscious than before he opened his mouth.

"Alright. I'll, uh, keep that in mind." She responded shyly. It was an awkward feeling. Speaking her mind was never a problem for her. It had been a very long time since a man had made her this kind of nervous. She tried to laugh off her nervousness and moved to continue their return to her office. "Um, we should get back and wrap up today's work so you can get back to the rest of your day. We accomplished a great deal today. And Anthony and I have a lot of material to work with. We'll be able to put together several options for you pretty quickly."

"The quicker the better." Dr. Ryan responded just as she walked past him through the door he held for her. Though tempted, Terry refused to look back at him. Keeping her eyes forward, she rushed to push the elevator button and whispered a "thank you" that the doors opened quickly.

"Did you say something?" Dr. Ryan asked.

Oh no, he heard me, she panicked a little.

"No, no." Now that the doors were closing, she was rethinking her gratitude. Mirrored elevator walls were not what you wanted in a moment like this. Think of something to say Terry, before he does. Ah!

"So, how well do you know Patrice Lewis? Have you worked with her long?"

Dr. Ryan's smile lit up the small mirrored space. "Nurse Lewis was a fixture at the hospital years before I joined the staff. She's a real sweetheart. She's one of those people that you look at and say there's no way that she's real. No one is that nice. But she really is."

By this time, the elevator had opened and released Terry onto her floor. Back in her domain, she felt more in control.

"I can definitely agree with that. She is a great person. In spite of the way it happened, I'm so glad we met." They entered her office and sat down.

"Oh? How did you meet?" Dr. Ryan's curiosity was piqued.

Terry offered him a bottle of water and carefully shared with him the events of the last week. Pointedly avoiding the embarrassing details of the story. He really didn't need to know those things anyway.

"Wow. You really have had a stressful week." Dr. Ryan commented. "More so than I thought. Just be sure to take care of yourself. I don't want you to have a repeat visit to the emergency room."

Terry had to look away. His demeanor had more than just a doctor's concern. Or did it? Either way, she wanted to keep her professional distance. At least for now. Again, she tried to laugh away her discomfort.

"I'm fine. Really. I have a better mental hold on several matters now. And through it all, I've gained a huge measure of peace and understanding about myself and how to handle things in my life that I didn't have before. Both physically and spiritually."

"Good. It's very important to be aware of both your physical and spiritual health. And I am a firm believer in prayer and meditation. For me, they are just as important as exercising the physical body." Dr. Ryan shared.

"You are so right. I don't know how I'd get through each week if I did not take my quiet time with God seriously. It has literally been my lifeline this week. There is no doubt about it. Those quiet moments have allowed me the space to clear some things out of my heart and mind that were a problem, a disappointment and just a block to my life's forward progression and happiness." By now, she was speaking more to herself than to her guest.

"I'll be sure not to disappoint you."

Dr. Ryan's words, though softly spoken, jolted Terry out of her reflective moment. This time when she looked up at him, it wasn't so easy to brush off what he said, how he said it or what she felt about it.

Realizing he had spoken his thoughts out loud, Dr. Ryan grabbed his water bottle and took a long swallow. But taking that moment still wasn't enough of a distraction. It was probably best that he leave before he really embarrassed himself. Can't start losing his cool points right away.

"Well. Um. I guess I'd better get going." He rose from his seat calmly and moved to retrieve his case and make his exit. His calm exterior couldn't hide his true discomfort. The fumbling with his jacket and his grip on his briefcase handle spoke the truth loud and clear.

"Ryan!?" Terry stood up to halt his retreat. But she had no words. At least not any that she felt safe letting flow from her lips. For him, at that moment, his name was enough. He liked the sound of her saying it.

"Terry, It's ok. You don't have to say anything." He took a deep breath, pasted on a smile and changed the subject. "It's been a very good day. I can't wait to see what you and Anthony put together. I'll give Evan a call tonight so that he's up to speed on everything."

"Ok. We'll get to work right away and give you a call." Terry relaxed a little. It helped that the source of her nervousness was about to walk out of the room.

"Great." Dr. Ryan stuck out his hand to shake hers.

Terry placed her hand in his, but quickly shook and then pulled her hand from his. Warm, soft and firm. In that short moment, she made a mental note to avoid physical contact with him until her emotions completely settled.

"Have a great afternoon Dr. Ryan."

"You know, Terry, we are going to be seeing quite a bit of each other. So please, just call me Ryan."

"Will do." Terry smiled shyly. Why on earth would such a simple thing feel like such a big deal to her? Taking away that small barrier of his title opened the door to a more relaxed atmosphere and she had to be careful. But, for right now, she simply agreed. Any protest on her part would surely drag out his departure. And she needed to gather her thoughts.

"Good. You have a great day. I'll talk to you soon." Ryan said his final goodbye and was out the door.

Terry plopped down on the sofa with a deep sigh. Giving deep thought to what was happening between her and Ryan, she tried to process her thoughts about this week out loud. "Heart break... well not really." She corrected herself. "An old flame. And now this strange beginning of something...new, sweet and nerve racking at the same time." She sat there shaking her head in pleasant wonderment. Life could certainly change drastically in a matter of days, moments even. Just then Her office phone rang bringing her mind back to the day at hand.

"Back to the grind." She quickly moved to answer the call.

CHAPTER TWENTY SEVEN

Shifting her mind back to work, she could focus her attention on everything except the good doctor. It was not easy, but necessary. The caller ID on her phone helped.

"Hello. What can I do for you Ms. Angela?" Terry answered the call, taking a seat to relax while she talked to her friend.

"Hey Hon. How are you doing today?" Angela brightly responded. But Terry could tell that something wasn't quite right. That cheery tone was forced.

"Hey? What's going on? Are you alright?" Terry quizzed.

"Yeah I'm ok. I just got back into the office from showing a potential client a few properties for a restaurant." Angela hesitated a moment before continuing. "There's just so much about him that feels strange."

"Hold up. You wait one minute. Don't tell me you were riding around with some weird or stalker type guy?" All professional tone left Terry's voice and she stood up in protest, ready to run to her friend's side. Too many things have happened recently for her to be nonchalant about something like this.

"No. No. You know my policy. We drove separately. But Terry, just being around this man puts me on edge." The level of agitation in her voice was escalating. "I'm probably overreacting but I can't help it."

"On edge? You need to do something about that. Why don't you have someone else work with him? If you are not feeling safe, just have David handle it." Terry took a deep breath and tried to calm down. No one messes with her Angela. "Angela, please don't make me go there again so soon. It's only been a few days since I had to threaten to shock a joker."

"Terry, wait! Now you are overreacting." Angela tried to talk Terry down.

"No. No I am not. You know I don't play when it comes to my momma, sister and my girls."

"Terry! Sweetheart! Please calm down! He is not causing me discomfort because he's dangerous. That's not it. Honey, he's actually the opposite."
"What?"

"Yeah. He's polite and well mannered and very professional. But he just reminds me so much of Carl, it's scary." Angela's voice trailed off in a near whisper.

"Ohh. Now I see. So this guy isn't really doing anything except reminding you of what you lost." Terry slowly sank back into her chair.

"Terry, I get this surreal feeling every time he walks into the room. I lost it the first time I met him." Angela confessed.

"Aww. Honey, I'm so sorry. But, like I said, just let David take over and free yourself from the stress. He's your number two there. He can handle it for you." Terry pressed.

"I can't. He specifically requested me. And besides, I'm not running away from my commission. It would be different if there was more pressing business that needed my attention. But it's just me freaking out a little. It's been so long and it was just hard seeing someone so much like Carl. It was a shock. But it's nothing compared to what you've been dealing with. So really. I'll be fine." She explained, trying to calm Terry.

"Angela, are you absolutely sure?"

"Yes I am. I can do all things, remember? Look, I just wanted to check in with you, not worry and unload on you. I'm really okay. It helped to talk things out so that I can actually hear my thoughts and how real my concerns may or may not be. And now that I've said it out loud, I think I'll be able to talk with Mr. Sinclair without being emotionally on edge." Angela tried to reassure her.

"Ok. If you are sure, I won't press the issue. But if anything goes awry, I'm calling David myself. You got me sister? You're not the only one that can put her foot down around here." Terry warned.

"I know, I know." Angela relented.

"And while I'm at it, I'm going to return to you some sound advice that you once gave to me. Remember," Terry warned, "do not let what seems familiar cause you to mistakenly see him in a role that is not his to play in your life. So don't expect this man to show up as your memories. Okay?"

"Yes ma'am. I hear you loud and clear. Thank you Terry. I knew you were the one to call. Love you Girl!" This time, Angela's voice was genuinely relaxed.

"I love you too." Terry replied, wiping away the tear that was trying to fall.

"Now, back to my original reason for calling. How are things going for you today? You sound good." Angela observed.

"Angela, you would not believe how great I am doing today." Terry started to feel giddy all over again. "And guess what!"

"Another guess what? Uh oh. Let me brace myself. What?"

"Remember I told you about Ryan yesterday?"

"Oh, it's Ryan now." Angela teased.

"Cut it out. Anyway, I found out today that his partner is the very high profile investor Anthony and I were hoping to connect with. Angela, this is major. Everything Evan touches turns to gold and we are now connected to one if his nuggets. I'm so excited." Before Angela could get out two words, Terry cut her off with the rest of her wonderful news. "Oh, and remember the contract I thought we lost? Girl, you will not believe this. They not only gave it to us, they nearly tripled the scope of the project as a whole. And the impact of the basic project was already going to skyrocket the reputation of our business to the next level."

"Wow! That's amazing! What do you think made them change everything?"

"God only knows. And I'm not questioning it. I'm just going to thank God for each of these awesome blessings." Terry offered as her explanation.

"Honey! That's all you can do. Now, look for what's next. You know how God does. I'm so glad things are getting back to normal and even better for you."

"Me too. And I feel like celebrating. So, did you talk to Leigh yet?" Terry shifted the conversation to one of her favorite things. Time with her girls.

"Oh yeah. You know she's ready. Got her wine selection and all." Angela joked and Terry joined in.

"Oh boy. I can't wait. The last time we were together things didn't turn out too good. So I'm going to enjoy our seafood feast to the fullest. I'll check with Krys again tomorrow to make sure she doesn't need anything from us."

"Alright then. Let me know. I'm going to let you get back to work.
Call me if you need anything. Love you."

"Love you too. I'll see you Saturday." Terry hung up and turned her
attention back to her computer.

CHAPTER TWENTY EIGHT

Terry felt like she was on top of the world. Looking at the materials from their meeting, her mind quickly slid into her creative zone. Before she knew it, an hour had gone by and Anthony was walking in with the Tadashi contract.

"Ok Terry. Chad just left. We are ready to go. So get your ink pen out."

"And we don't need to change anything?" She questioned.

"Believe it or not, no we don't. Chad looked over everything. Terry, as you read, they made this contract specific to us. You and me. Why they would do that, I don't know. This is basically our contract. That also means we bare all of the responsibility. But the terms are fair and we are going to be paid very well for our work. So let's just get this thing finalized."

"Alright. Hand it over. Let's do this!" Terry push the button to call Kayla and asked her to bring her notary stamp in. She took her favorite pen and signed both copies of the contract and handed them over to Kayla to notarize and prepare the appropriate copies.

"I'll be right back." Anthony disappeared through the door without a second glance. Satisfied that things were on track, She shrugged off his disappearing act and turned back to her computer screen. But as soon as Kayla returned, Anthony appeared, hot on her heels with his briefcase, keys and shades.

"Uh, going somewhere?" Terry asked with raised brows.

"Yes ma'am. Making a delivery. I'm going to see to it myself that this envelope makes it to Tadashi's office." He announced and Terry immediately backed him.

"Then I'll get Kayla to notify Karen and email an electronic copy over. Call me when you leave there." She ordered.

"No problem. Give me the set that needs to go." Terry handed him the stack of copies for him to look through. Satisfied that he had to correct original and supporting copies, Anthony slid the stack into the large envelope and secured it in his briefcase. "Alright. I'm out of here. I'll call after I make the delivery." Not waiting for a response, Anthony grabbed his keys from the desk and left.

Terry took the moment to whisper another thank you. She was still so amazed at how this day was turning out.

Thirty-five minutes later, Anthony called to let her know that he had successfully made his delivery. "Tadashi happened to call while I was there. And of course, Karen let him know that I was there to bring back the signed contract. Terry, he actually asked to speak to me." He told her, revealing his surprise.

Perplexed, Terry asked, "What's so strange about that. You are going to be working with him very heavily over the next year, and then beyond. That's not so strange."

"Terry, the one time he actually even attempted to hold a conversation with me past asking me to have you call him, he took that opportunity to very nicely let me know that he expected to only deal with the decision maker. You. Men like that don't just change. There's something to this. Just keep your eyes open." Anthony tried to convince her that his caution was justified. They had a good thing here but that was no excuse for not paying attention to the details. But Terry tried to put his mind at ease.

"Anthony, I don't know what the change of heart is about, but we are well able to handle the demands of this job. So, as long as we take care of our business, we will be just fine. No matter what."

"You're right." Anthony agreed. "Listen Terry, since it's so late, I'm going to handle a couple of things outside of the office. So I won't be back today."

"Ok. That's fine by me. We just need to make sure that we are ready to get started on the Tadashi account first thing Tomorrow. I'll prep some things before I leave today. See you in the morning."

"Later." And then he was gone. Terry wondered only a little bit about what he had to do. She intentionally tried to stay out of his "free" time.

CHAPTER TWENTY NINE

Terry left the office only fifteen minutes past her normal time but it cost her twenty extra minutes on the drive home. Pulling up to her house, she saw Leighann get out of her car with a bag to walk into her open garage door. By the time the garage door closed behind Terry's car, Leighann was already upstairs moving things around in her kitchen.

"Chica! Get in here girl. I hear we have something big to celebrate and I'm not waiting until Saturday!" Leighann announced as she was pulling the cork from the wine bottle.

"Leigh, I just got off and you're already trying to sauce me up. Can I change and put some food on my stomach? Something?" Terry protested through her laughter.

"Go ahead. But I'm not waiting for you."

"I wouldn't think of such a thing." Terry threw over her shoulder as she went upstairs.

Tossing her briefcase on the bed she went to her walk in and put on her favorite short romper. She loved how it made her feel. Cute and comfy, all at the same time.

"Girl, you're taking too long up there!" Leighann called up.

"Relax child. I'll be down in a minute." Terry slid into her slippers and headed back down to her friend who promptly handed her a half full glass. Terry stopped and lifted the glass with a swirl, and looked back at Leighann.

"You're not wasting my wine. That's about all you drink anyway, so keep it moving." Leighann shot back, moving to take her seat at the table.

"So really, you brought the wine for you. But the rest of the spread is for me." Terry surmised, sitting across from her friend.

"A little something for you, little sip for me. And of course, you get to see my beautiful face. It's a win win situation. Never waste a celebration." Leighann raised her glass and took another sip.

"What in the world am I going to do with you?" Terry asked, shaking her head.

"Well, right now, you are going to tell me all about your good news. And don't leave out a thing about the cute doctor Angela mentioned. By the way, good move. Don't let THE grass grow under your feet. You have to let that buster know that you are not at a loss because of him. Get back up on that horse and ride Sally ride!" Leighann finished with her arm waving in the air.

"Leigh! Ain't nobody riding nothing around here." Terry tried to stop her antics. "It's nothing like that. I don't know what Angela told you, but Ryan is my client and there will be no "riding" going on. I'm a professional. Okay?"

"Mm hm. We'll see." Leighann took another sip to that.

"Good grief child. Give me a break please." Terry popped a piece of fruit in her mouth, shaking her head in exasperation.

"Alright then," Leighann sat up straight, crossed her legs and arms, while balancing her glass between her fingers, "tell me what happened at the office today."

Terry rolled her eyes. "You know you're something else, right?"

"Of course," Leighann responded matter of factly.

"Okay. I just wanted to make sure you knew that." Terry went on to explain how Ryan was connected to Evan Blake and what that meant. And then halfway through telling her about the Tadashi contract, her doorbell rang.

When she opened the door, she was totally surprised to see Anthony standing there with a vase of flowers.

"Hey? What's going on? Come on in." Anthony handed her the flowers as he walked by.

"I was going to have these delivered tomorrow but I thought, what the heck. So here I am."

"Thank you. But what's the occasion? One of your things to do this afternoon didn't mess us up did it?" Terry asked suspiciously.

"No. Not at all."

"Hey. Is that An-thony I hear?" Leighann came spying around the corner.

"What's up Leigh? I was just making a congratulatory delivery and my partner here is looking at me like I did something wrong." He looked at Terry side eyed.

"Well, Terry, you could hear him out before you start pointing fingers." Leighann defended him.

"Look who's talking. I have guilty and guiltier standing before me." Terry shot back.

"Well, that's my cue. I'm outta here. Talk to you later Leighann." Anthony gave Leighann a quick hug and then turned to Terry. "I just wanted to bring you something nice to show my appreciation for the hard work you've done at the office, say congratulations on our victories today, and just because you're a great friend who's come through a lot this week. I'll see you in the morning. Have a great night."

"Night Anthony." Anthony gave her a hug before he walked out of the door. He didn't do it too often, but like any other time he did, she felt comforted. But he, on the other hand, noticed more than he ever did. The scent of the lotion she applied earlier was still present, and the touch of her hand on his back felt warm. When he released her, he glanced only briefly in Leighann's direction before bolting through the doorway. His mind was racing. "What's wrong with me," he thought to himself as he walked down the stairs, pausing momentarily at the bottom to look back at the door that just closed. Shaking his head to clear his thoughts, he jumped in his car and sped off.

When Terry walked back into the kitchen, Leighann was standing by the sink, running her fingers around the rim of her refilled wine glass. Looking up as Terry entered, Leighann bluntly confessed, "Terry, I really like him. I know I'm not the type he usually dates. But I think I'm going to give it a try and let him know."

Terry stopped in her tracks and stood in stunned silence. When she could move again, finding her voice, she whispered, "Oh no, we really are about to enter the twilight zone. For real," before taking a gulp from her glass.

"Huh? You say something?" Her companion asked distractedly.

"Nope." Terry replied, slowly shaking her head in bewilderment. "Drink your wine Leighann. Just drink your wine."

Discussion Questions

1. Which character stood out the most to you and why?

2. Did you personally identify with a particular character?

3. Who are the people that bring out the Angela and Leighann in you?

4. There are several types of interpersonal connections represented in this book. Have you ever experienced a connection with someone that surprised you?

5. Have you had a time in your life that seemed to take your breath away? How did you get through that tough time in your life?

6. Who or what is your "safe place," voice of reason and comfort?

7. Have you ever had a discovery moment with your parent? Did this moment have a positive or negative effect on your relationship?

8. Share an instance of self discovery that changed your outlook about who you are. Did it make you cry or laugh?

9. How easy do you forgive others? Yourself?

10. What lesson(s) or helpful advice can you take away from this book?

Author: Bernadette Williams

Contact:
Taylour Mayde Publishing, LLC
802-444-1867
TaylourMaydePub@gmail.com